Northern Comfort
The Musings of Jacqueline Pine Savage

Northern Comfort
The Musings of Jacqueline Pine Savage

Jodi Schwen

NORTH STAR PRESS OF ST. CLOUD, INC.
St. Cloud, Minnesota

Dedication

I'd like to thank all my family and friends who looked the other way when I jotted down yet another foible, faux pas, or frivolity as future story material. Even when they learned that it might end up in print, they didn't run when they saw me coming and loved me anyway. I especially owe a huge debt of gratitude to my husband, Kent, and our sons, Andy, David, and Nick (who are called "Jack," "the saplings," or "Wee Jack" in these pages). I love you more than you know.

Copyright © 2014 Jodi Schwen

Cover art by David Schwen

ISBN: 978-0-87839-734-1

All rights reserved.

First Edition: June 2014

Printed in the United States of America

Published by
North Star Press of St. Cloud, Inc.
P.O. Box 451
St. Cloud, Minnesota 56302

northstarpress.com

Spring

❧ True Confessions ❧

Spring means new beginnings—Easter, cleaning out winter's cobwebs, 'fessing up to the sins of one's youth—all the things we do in the heady impetuosity of youth, then pray our parents won't find out. By the time you finish reading this, I may be grounded and, believe me, it's long overdue.

What prompted this angst of the soul? Once, as I pondered the cherubic faces of our sons, I wondered what secrets lurked behind those innocent countenances. I would never be allowed passage into the secrets of their childhood escapades—simply because many of their infractions haven't yet exceeded the statute of limitations beyond which said crime is unpunishable.

In other words, they could still be taken out to the woodshed.

First, a disclaimer: My shenanigans are small potatoes. I want to take our collective minds off the tragedies we see on the evening news. Let's remember a simpler time, when living dangerously meant going swimming as soon as one pushed away from the dinner table.

I'll begin somewhat chronologically. I once made up a story about seeing the Easter Bunny running up the hill after it had supposedly visited our house. At Christmastime, I tried to move a bayberry-scented book from my little sister's Santa pile to mine. My parents have probably already sorted fact from fiction in those cases.

My sister, Sara, and I sneaked sweets from the breakfast table when Mom wasn't looking—a swipe of creamy butter, a spoon licked and dipped repeatedly into the sugar bowl, a few spoonsful of jelly. I removed the safety flag from my bike and hid it in the bushes at the end of the driveway. I hitched a forbidden ride to the Dairy Queen with a neighbor girl whose ink was barely dry on her driver's license. In the late 1960s, I rolled up my skirts to a more fashionable length, hiding the excess under a bulky sweater or tucked under my wide leather belt.

I was busted often enough to keep me relatively honest. I tried the old, "Ask Mother, Ask Father," scam when I wanted to go swimming at a friend's house—and got caught—and grounded. I ate the chocolate candy bar (I was allergic to chocolate) at the elementary school Christmas party. I told my parents we were given candy canes. How was I to know that my father's Kiwanis Club provided the treats that year? Knowing my allergy, he probably tried to do me a favor and steered the vote toward hard candy.

The only time I played hooky in my entire educational career was when I ditched piano lessons at the ripe old age of eight. I dutifully walked across the street from my elementary school to the home of the elderly piano teacher, dragged myself up her front porch steps, and lifted a reluctant hand to knock very quietly on the door. I convinced myself no one was home and left. I've often wondered if they still had to pay her for the missed lesson.

But the *pièce de résistance* involves a one-piece swimsuit and a handful of forbidden pre-supper cookies. Back in the olden days of one-bra-size-fits-all swimsuits, I had a blue, stretchy, polyester number, and my budding figure didn't quite do it justice. I was in the kitchen sneaking cookies before supper when I heard Mom coming. Caught cookie-handed, I became extremely resourceful—as children do when cornered—and shoved them down the roomy top of my swimsuit. Exiting quickly with cookies crumbling against my chest, I removed myself to my room where I could retrieve and eat them in peace.

And last but not least, there was the time, years ago, I found myself dragged onstage with a troupe of male dancers. A friend (who was also an upstanding citizen—and our church secretary) and I had joined the studio audience at an innocent taping of the former Twin Cities television show, *Good Company*. It had been held on location in the Brainerd area at a resort on the shores of Gull Lake to kick off fishing opener weekend.

I must have looked like a good sport. During the performance, I was scooped out of my chair by an extremely muscular, half-dressed man, and deposited onstage to enjoy the rest of the show. I blushed profusely, relieved I could hide behind the anonymity of my sunglasses. Thankfully, that portion of the pre-taped show ended up on the cutting-room floor. How would I have explained *that* episode to my husband?

They say that confession is good for the soul. I challenge you to come clean. Break out in a rash of confessions and get the cookies off your chest. I know I feel better.

∽ Howl Together ∽
Or
Some of what I know about marriage I learned from my dogs

Our dog had her honeymoon the same time as Jack and I had ours. Jack already owned Nikki, an Alaskan malamute, when we met. We decided to breed her with Jack's brother's malamute, Nanook. All his brother wanted in exchange was the male pick-of-the-litter. He left Nanook with us when he came to the wedding. We settled in, and the dogs got acquainted.

What we forgot to tell Nanook was that Nikki already had a boyfriend in the neighborhood—a wimpy husky named Pasha. We kept Nikki tied up, but there was no need to tie Nanook. He wasn't about to abandon his bride to the tender ministrations of the local talent. Poor Pasha. He was out-weighed, out-manuevered, out-everythinged by Nanook. One fierce altercation of flying fur and flashing teeth, and Pasha limped home to whine from afar for the duration of the malamutes' courtship. Though their future dates were restricted to holidays and family gatherings, in our eyes, Nikki and Nanook were considered old married folk.

Always having been a dog-person, I can attribute some of what I've learned about marriage to the dogs in my life.

Lesson 1: Mate for Life. "Till death do us part" has been the promise of all the great romances throughout history: Romeo and Juliet, Jack and Jacqueline, Sam and Jinni . . . let me explain the last one.

When I was a girl, long before Hollywood immortalized the Saint Bernard in the *Beethoven* movies, there was Jinni, my mother's Saint. Jinni joined our canine family as a clumsy companion for Sam, our golden retriever. What we never expected was the way he would take her under his wing and try to teach her everything he knew—including swimming.

Sam, the veteran water-dog, took Jinni down to the dock soon after her arrival. Looking back, it could almost have been an initiation or a hazing for the new dog on the block. Sam took a confident flying leap off the end of the dock into ten feet of water. Without pausing to consider the risks, Jinni followed, but she was instantly dragged to the bottom by her heavy coat of puppy fur. Dad pulled her out before she drowned.

Despite her near-drowning, Sam and Jinni remained inseparable. If we wanted to keep Jinni home, we tied up Sam. (How that analogy fits with Jack and me, I'm not exactly sure—stay with me on this one.) When Sam died, Jinni went on a hunger strike. All she would eat was canned Chef Boy-ar-dee spaghetti, and only if we hand-fed her. The *Beethoven* movies had the slobber scenes right—slime didn't begin to describe my hands after coaxing her to eat canned spaghetti.

Like Sam and Jinni, Jack and I are a team. While helping me prepare for a garage sale, our saplings discovered Jack's little black book in a musty cardboard box dragged down from the rafters. The kids were old enough to comprehend the significance of their find, yet young enough to think it slightly dangerous. I assured them it contained the also-rans, the wannabes, and—judging from the dust on the cover—hardly posed a threat to our marriage. Just as old inscriptions in our high school yearbooks and on the backs of graduation photos had been chuckled over and then forgotten, so too were these names and numbers.

Lesson 2: Howl together. Sam also taught Jinni to howl. Saint Bernards aren't normally howlers, but when Sam serenaded Jinni, she answered, and their unlikely duet echoed hauntingly into the night. The night Sam died, Jinni began a soft howl on her own, but when Sam didn't respond, she never howled again.

Jack and I don't exactly howl, but I have surprised him a time or two to keep our marriage interesting. I once sent the kids to Grandpa's house and drove myself to the motel where Jack was staying on business. It was fun to see his face when he opened the door at 10:30 p.m., but it was even more fun checking out the next morning, and explaining to the clerk that I really was his wife.

Lesson 3: When life stinks, head for home. When Nikki had her puppies, we kept a female and named her Kina. Nikki was a saint in her own way. Now long deceased, her legacy over the years has been elevated to that of perfect dog, in all areas but one. Malamutes like to run and Nikki was no exception. The road near our home leads to a swamp, and if Nikki led Kina astray, we knew they'd head for the swamp. They would eventually come out on an adjoining road, reached by a circuitous route via the highway—five minutes one way.

I tell you this because it was Jack's turn to find them after one of their escapades. I knew something was wrong when he sped home in our full-sized van, and peeled into our driveway on two wheels. Jumping out, he threw the side door open, hollering, "They got skunked!" Our Italian neighbor mourned the waste of my home-canned tomato juice.

Nikki and Kina weren't the only ones who got skunked. Remember the brother who wanted the pick-of-the-litter male? Nikki only had three puppies—all females. Jack and I are still together, but Nikki might have had better luck with Pasha.

The Welcome Mat

The house tour is greatly over-rated. You know the drill. Before having company over for dinner, the whole house has to be cleaned from top to bottom, because sooner or later your guests will ask the dreaded, age-old question: "Can we see the rest of the house?" I hold with the military's premise of "need-to-know." All my guests really need to know—other than where I hid their coats—is "Top of the stairs, first door on the left."

When did the Great American House Tour become popular?

The one-room log cabin, or the even earlier one-room soddy, precluded the need for a house tour. It was the forerunner of the cliché, "What you see, is what you get." A house tour was unnecessary because the whole family lived, slept, and ate together in one room. The farmer might ask, "Do you want to go see the new calf?" Then the menfolk would traipse out to visit the barn, while the womenfolk took out their knitting—the guest nodding approval of what the Missus had done with her limited space and resources. Little decorating touches such as a rag rug, a neatly swept dirt floor, or a window carved out of the sod wall went a long way in those days.

But once the Missus outgrew her cramped quarters, she pestered her Mister for another room. A two-room soddy was a novelty. Neighbor women from miles around showed up to gape at the entrance to the second room, even though it held the identical fixtures as the single room. It was the curiosity factor. Myriad questions begged answers: "Along which wall did Constance place the trundle bed? Where did she hang the clothes pegs?" And above all, "How can I get my Mister to build me one o' these?" We've been suffering the consequences ever since.

Perhaps the inbred fear of inspection is the reason my hospitality skills are so dusty. Granted, my house could stand a good going-over. One of our children has allergies. I recently read an article detailing ways to allergy-proof my house—little things like cleaning under my kitchen sink weekly using a chlorine bleach solution (have I ever cleaned under my kitchen sink?) and washing our clothes in a lethal water temperature of 130 degrees (that would shrink the winter woolens, you betcha).

The article also recommended keeping the pets off the beds. No pets? Not a chance! In Minnesota, we need those furry critters for warmth. (Haven't you heard of the Three Dog Night?) The article also mentioned storing items in the attic. Do you have an attic? I don't. When did we decide crawl spaces were more cost effective? By the way, the allergy study was published in New York City—making its conclusions more-than-slightly suspect.

I lived in the same house for the first eighteen years of my life. Come to think of it, that house didn't have an attic, either. When my parents decided to move, we spent untold hours finishing all the little touches necessary for attracting potential buyers. By the time the house sold, it was so perfect, I wished we could stay. That lesson apparently didn't sink in, because as young-marrieds, Jack and I decided to move into our house before it was completed. We would finish it as we had time/money/energy. I'm still waiting. I can be oblivious to the chaos around me until I think about entertaining guests, Then my projects reach out and hit me in the face—little things that we overlook when it's just us.

• Our fourth bedroom reaching completion in time for Wee Jack's arrival—sixteen years later.

• The downstairs bath relegated to the boys and, therefore, *never* recommended to guests.

• The ironing piling up for so long it needs re-laundering, or at least dusting. I once was tempted to take a friend's suggestion and avoid ironing altogether by taking my clothes to the consignment store. The only catch was they would refuse my contributions because they weren't ironed.

My house had become my excuse. Instead of getting it in tip-top shape, I lamented its shortcomings and never entertained. Or at least never entertained people whose homes I knew were better than mine. I've now concluded that if everyone in the Midwest who felt their homes weren't good enough for a centerfold in *Better Homes and Gardens* raised their hands, the warm breeze those waving arms generated would hasten the spring thaw.

Come on over. You're welcome anytime, if you don't look in the closets or under the sink. And remember—top of the stairs, first door on the left.

A Mother's Day Lament

Whose bright idea was it to place the Minnesota fishing opener on Mother's Day weekend? I long for a lovingly prepared breakfast in bed, leisurely late church service, followed by a sumptuous twenty-foot-long buffet enjoyed in the bosom of my adoring family. Instead, I get a cold bed because Jack went fishing at 3:00 a.m. Breakfast is dry toast lovingly prepared by our kids, whom I have to hustle to church solo, while mediating the bickering over who gets to sit in the front seat—which in the era of air bags may not be such a prime location. My buffet consists of cheese and macaroni. When Jack's gone, I don't have to cook.

Some think Mother's Day is just another opportunity for Hallmark to rake in the cash for sappy sentimental cards. Jack takes this view: "You're not my mother. Why do I have to get you a card?" Perhaps to set a good example for our Jackpine Savage saplings? Nonetheless, I always buy his mother a card.

I'd like to meet the bureaucrat in the upper echelons of the Department of Natural Resources who thought he'd placate Minnesota mothers by tossing them a freebie. (Normally I'm a sucker for anything I don't have to pay for—not this time.) "I know," he said. "We'll still put fishing opener on Mother's Day weekend, but we'll let all the little mothers fish free on Mother's Day." I wonder if his own mother is still speaking to him?

I'm sorry, but that's like playing a carnival game and winning the cracked plastic bird whistle from under the counter, when you had your heart set on the five-foot, pink, stuffed panda hanging from the marquee.

Aren't we worth the panda? Is one day of unadulterated worship too much to ask? Mothers are more than just women who give birth. We're the chief cooks and bottle-washers, the ones who stock up on toothpaste and toilet paper—and most importantly, the finders of things invisible to any naked eye but our own.

I wish video technology had been invented when Jack and I got married. I'd play the vows backwards to discover the hidden message where I'd promised to love, honor, and be the Keeper of the Stuff.

There is one person in every household who always knows where an item can be found on any given day. Nine times out of ten, it's the mother. I'm not a neat-freak with a blueprint for a brain, but I either know exactly where to find the warranty for the bug-zapper we bought five years ago, or I can tell you two alternate locations, one of which is sure to be pay dirt.

"Where are my keys?" Jack hollers thirty seconds before going out the door.

"Where-did-you-put-them?" I reply in auto-replay mode. Does he think I take pleasure in hiding his stuff? Is there a sadistic joy in knowing he is totally dependent on my producing the keys so he won't be late for work?

His voice rises to a frenzied pitch: "They're not there." I wearily walk over to the counter, move aside one of the scraps of paper that he'd deposited along with his keys, and *voila*, there they are.

"Just because they didn't pop out and say 'Here I am,'" I mutter, as he scoops them up and dashes out the door.

This pattern repeats itself with clothes on his side of the closet, "Where's my plaid shirt?" and condiments in the refrigerator, "Have you seen the barbecue sauce?" My personal favorite is, "Who hid the TV remote?" I did, of course. When my last afternoon soap opera was over, I shoved it into the bon-bon box and slid it under the couch.

Being a fishing wife is trial enough. Don't expect me to fish. I'm still trying to calculate how long I have to keep the leeches in the back of the refrigerator before I can justify throwing them out. Like leftovers, they're never used again. They just take up valuable shelf space as they slowly grow fuzzy little sweaters.

Maybe this May, when the ice goes off the lake and his thoughts turn to jigs and lures, I can finally turn the whole situation to my advantage.

"Jackie, have you seen my tackle box?"

"Tackle box? Gee, dear, I don't know. Where did you put it?"

Bargain Basement
Brotherhood

There is a clandestine movement underway in Minnesota and beyond. It isn't identified by a fancy name with a memorable acronym. It doesn't have a secret handshake, standard uniform, or even a strict meeting schedule. Nevertheless, its members recognize each other by sight (though they may not know each other's names), vital information pertinent to their cause is often exchanged, and they frequently induct like-minded friends or relatives into their membership. In this club, bankers and lawyers rub elbows with stay-at-home moms and college students. They are spotted milling around at garage sales, thrift and secondhand stores, consignment shops, used book sales, flea markets, and auctions. Believe me, I know. I'm a charter member.

I'm not quite sure when I officially joined their ranks. My early interest was sparked when my mother took me to the Nisswa flea market and the first few antique shops in Crosby. The flames were fanned even further when Jack and I were newlyweds and we gratefully furnished our first house with family hand-me-downs and college apartment leftovers. It continued as a steady glow when I decided I didn't want to spend my hard-earned money on a maternity wardrobe that I'd wear for a mere few months. The fire was continually fed when our saplings were wee sprouts and grew out of their baby clothing faster than a tamarack sheds its needles. Whatever sparked the frugal Scandinavian within me, I was hooked for life.

So it started with hand-me-downs: why buy baby or toddler clothes new when friends with children a little older than mine, were willing to hand-'em-down? And when the same friends were no longer wearing maternity clothing, they were more than happy to "hand-'em-up." (Actually it was more like: "I can't stand the sight of these any longer—please, take them, wear them. I hope I never need them again!") And furnishing our new love nest with gently used pieces from garage sales and thrift stores became an adventure.

"Honey, guess what I found today?" I said, trying to shield the "new" recliner behind my back. Jack's reply was usually a variation of the theme: "Where did you unearth this chair/table/doohickey, and how long will it take you to put mine back?"

That's the true beauty/risk of secondhand shopping. The sales are always final. The good news is that if a purchase is truly a decorating disaster, you can put it in your own garage sale later and recoup your losses.

I can't speak for the others in my scavenger clan, but I've found some really great, dirt-cheap stuff in highly unlikely places, such as:

• A 1965 Superball just like the one I lost on the bus when I was in elementary school. I'll never know which fellow rider pocketed it, but I have my suspicions.

• On the opposite end of the spectrum: A turquoise silk, knock 'em dead, slinky Liz Claiborne dress.

• An antique table with four leaves and six chairs—newly recovered and refinished. Good thing, too, since we all know how handy I would be at that sort of crafty undertaking.

- Too many books to count—yet somehow never enough to adequately feed my craving. We bookaholics firmly believe that the one who dies with the most books wins.

The only downside to this shopping malady occurs when Minnesota temperatures plummet and half of our favorite venues (garage sales, auctions, flea markets) shut down for the winter. To prevent suffering cold-turkey withdrawal during the winter months, alternate stop-gap bargain hunting methods are frequently employed, such as shopping Goodwill, Salvation Army, the occasional library used-book sale, and Facebook online garage sale groups.

Forget robins. The true sign of spring is sighting the first garage sale sign sprouting along the highway.

I may put my membership in jeopardy by revealing all the truly fantastic bargains that can be uncovered in Lake Country. But just remember, if you and I turn up at a sale together and we both head for the puce loveseat and matching ottoman—I saw it first.

FAFSA
Another Word for Headache

Back to school evokes sweet memories of timid kindergartners climbing mountainous school-bus steps for the first time. All they'll need for survival (PB&J sandwich, milk money, jumbo crayons, and white paste derived from horses' hooves) is stored in bookbags strapped like harnesses to their skinny backs. At day's end, the buses creep like giant caterpillars along country roads, depositing their charges back home. Mother hovers solicitously, camera clicking to document Junior/Juniorette's first tentative steps up the thirteen-grade pecking order.

Her young saplings will discover that some kids are bigger and pushier, and not everything served in the lunchroom even remotely resembles lunch, but even then most crises can be whittled down to size over a plate of chocolate chip cookies and a glass of milk.

Enjoy the early years. By the time they are seniors, a handful of cookies will no longer fill them up, let alone ease the Senior Debt. I'll never forget when our first strapping sapling graduated from high school before branching out into the Real Forest. The following is a crash course on what to expect when your adorable wee sprout reaches the top of the gold-plated Senior Year Totem Pole.

Forget the advice about financial planning for college expenses—you'd better toss a pile of extra money into the kitty for senior year. If your senior only works a summer job, it's impossible to eke out his/her earnings for the full year's events. Sooner or later the Parent National Bank (or second mortgage, depending on your circumstances) will need to be tapped. There are the obvious excesses, such as $2,000 prom: limousine, designer ball gown, tuxedo, flowers, dinner at Posh on Main, prom pictures, and the day-after excursion down the Mississippi on a riverboat.

Graduation pictures are also more excessive than when we were kids. The hardest decision I made as a graduate was deciding between the pale-blue blouse and the red one. Outdoor pictures were just beginning to be in fashion when I graduated, but no one ever wore more than one outfit. Now kids opt for wardrobe changes, indoor/outdoor scenes, poses with boy/girl friends (what do you do if you break up before the photos are developed?), the family dog/cat/horse, sporting equipment, and/or musical instrument.

One of the largest black holes of senior-year spending is "Miscellaneous," the little expenses that crop up five minutes before your child heads out the door.

"Mom, I need $27.50/$45/$23.90/$18.95 for cap and gown, or yearbook, or Senior Tea [tea?], or Grad Blast." Senior expenses are lurking out there to get you when you least expect them, and/or when your checking account balance is $3.82 (not counting the spare change at the bottom of your purse or in the couch cushions). I've given up balancing my budget and I suggest you do the same. Make friends with your friendly bank/credit union—you're going to need them.

Which brings me to college financial planning.

When our sapling was a junior, the mother of a senior told me to have our taxes ready early next year. "Why?" I asked innocently. "FAFSA," was all she could utter before a shudder of revulsion spread over her face. It's the "Free Application for Federal Student Aid," which you fill out and file every year your student attends college—the earlier the better. Not only does this rub my procrastinating ways the wrong way, doing taxes in tandem with filling out the FAFSA was a double "please pass the Excedrin" whammy.

According to the Paperwork Reduction Act of 1995, completing this form shouldn't take longer than an hour and a half—including the time to "review instructions, search existing data resources, gather the data, and complete and review the information collection." It gives an address to send your comments regarding the time requirements. Do you think they'd understand "Aaaarrrggghh!"? We did ours on the Internet. It was a bonding experience between my sapling and me—akin to labor without the bundle of joy at the end.

The mailbox of the college-bound is stuffed with college brochures—and Uncle Sam also weighs in with military enlistment enticements to "be all you can be." The ensuing college visits pull the final plug on the budget drain. Weed out the "maybes" from the "must sees" ahead of time to reduce the college visitation equation: Airfare + Gas + Food + Motel x Number of Colleges = Big Bucks.

Maybe in writing about this, I can recoup a fraction of our losses. According to Philip Roth: "We writers are lucky: nothing truly bad can happen to us. It's all material."

I'll bet Roth never had a senior.

～ Checkmate ～

It's good to drag one's spouse out of his or her comfort zone every now and then—even if he or she is kicking and screaming. A few years ago, Jack was so busy with business trips and hunting—not necessarily in that order—I felt like I lived with a stranger I'd hardly seen in a month.

One morning, while I was listening to a radio station's bargain-shopping program, I heard them announce a radio coupon for a half-price special at a local bed and breakfast. From years of coupon-clipping habit I automatically reached for my scissors, then remembered it was a radio coupon. I picked up the phone and purchased the mid-week evening's stay—committing Jack and me to our first-ever night in the luxury suite of a bed and breakfast. I was excited. Jack's response was less than excited.

"A bed and breakfast? What will we do there? Will we have to eat with a bunch of strangers? I can't take time off from work!"

I was already several steps ahead of him.

"It's only half an hour away—you won't miss work. We are served a deluxe breakfast in the breakfast nook in the privacy of our own room." Then I played my trump card. "If you can't make it—I'll have to go by myself." He suddenly decided it was in his best interests to go with me. He knew if he were left home alone with the saplings, he'd have to cook supper and get them off to school in the morning. If we both went, we could leave them with the grandparents.

As I packed, I considered whether I should let Jack know that the room didn't come with a television and DVD player. His idea of a relaxing night is to fall asleep in front of the television watching a movie with an exciting chase scene. Having the guy chase, and catch, the girl apparently doesn't qualify. I usually vote for something with a plot. I decided to save the television surprise for later—much later—like after we'd checked in and it was too late for him to back out.

We had a leisurely drive to the charming vintage home. I was impressed with the immaculately kept grounds, tiny welcoming electric candles lit in every window, and the gracious demeanor of our host and hostess. We were the only guests so far that evening, which was a good thing. Jack could have bolted and fled if the living room had been packed with strangers with whom he would have been forced to meet and mingle.

Our suite of rooms consisted of a beautiful entryway, bathroom and dressing area, and a massive bedroom suite with a dining nook. In one corner, where a television entertainment center would have stood, was a chess table. It was the only thing that could have safely taken the place of a television set. Jack and I had often played chess when we were dating. My brother had taught me how to play when I was younger, and though I never mastered the strategy of the game, at least I knew how the pieces moved. However, I am still tempted to call the "rook" a "castle," and the "knight" a "horse." It was Jack's opportunity to beat me at chess once again—actually several times over the course of the evening—that made the lack of a television set permissible.

Strong, hot coffee was waiting by the door when we awoke—followed by a huge breakfast with at least a dozen different selections. There was so much food, we couldn't finish it all. If the way to a Jackpine Savage's heart is through his stomach, this establishment succeeded.

I don't know if I'll ever get Jack into another bed and breakfast. I think he's waiting for someone to design his idea of the perfect B&B. Motel rooms—with the remote screwed handily onto the bedside table—come close. But there must be more, much more. It must have a mammoth-screen TV and a Lazy-Man recliner equipped with a built-in refrigerator, well-stocked with delicacies like pickled pork hocks, pickled herring, and pickled just-about-anything-else. The remote would have a preprogrammed speed-dial system for channel surfing—racing past anything resembling a chick-flick, and automatically pausing on blood, sweat, cars, and testosterone. If there were such a place, Jack would be its best customer. But I think he already has one—it's called home.

Thoughts While Spring Cleaning

What is the statute of limitations on how long I'm required to store a grown child's possessions? Not that I'm eager to see the items go. Once they do, it means he'll never come home to live again, but will only drop by for occasional visits before returning to his own place. While it's a bittersweet thought, I could use the extra space.

I seem to have closets filled with items that aren't mine, but I don't dare dispose of them. A few items in the closet of our oldest departed sapling include: a Little League jersey, now several sizes too small; cassette tapes, obsolete in the advent of CDs and MP3s; a space-themed pencil box; a birdhouse he constructed in junior-high shop class; several thermal mugs stamped with the high school he attended; and a lime-green fanny pack—also a letter jacket that was required apparel for high school, but no one would be caught dead wearing on a college campus.

When I left home for good, I even took my childhood collection of Nancy Drew mysteries. I grew up with Nancy Drew—where wonderfully spooky houses had attics filled with exotic trunks waiting to be discovered. If the trunks didn't hold a clue to the latest mystery, they contained vintage clothing, floppy hats, and feather boas. The closest thing to a feather boa in my attic/crawl space, would be draping my neck with a strip of pink fiberglass insulation. I think that's why the packed closets bother me so much—our house doesn't have a large mysterious attic to accommodate the things we no longer need.

Jack still occasionally wonders what happened to some things from his childhood—his Lionel train set or his baseball-card collection. I can picture his mother on a cleaning binge, filling a box for the charity drive or to give to the children next door. I've done it myself—we only have so much space. Bringing in more stuff, without disposing of some of the old, would cause the house to burst at the seams. Mothers nationwide carry a lingering burden of guilt for having given away the Mickey Mantle cards now worth thousands of dollars, which somehow landed in the possession of antique dealers. Rare is the person whose home includes a warehouse or a barn spacious enough to store all that good stuff until its antique value kicks in.

What prairie housewife could have dreamed that the Calumet baking powder tin sitting on her rustic kitchen shelf would one day be worth ten times its contents? Which brings me to my "Top Ten List for Future Antiques."

1. Altoids tins: Especially the tiny ones. Don't throw them away, ever. My collection already threatens to avalanche from the top shelf.

2. Plastic milk jugs: Look what happened to their predecessor, the glass milk jug. No one thought they were valuable either. Even more valuable will be ones with the plastic opening strips still attached to the caps. But don't try to save them unopened—that only works with Wheaties.

3. Cassette tapes and players: Like eight-tracks before them, cassettes are destined to be the collectibles of the future.

4. Old lipstick tubes and deodorant bottles: Think about it. No one ever saves these—they are certain to achieve valued antique status.

5. Irons: Either clothing will become so advanced that wrinkles become obsolete or we'll be so busy that wrinkled clothing becomes a status symbol.

6. TV remotes: When science produces an electronic TV guide with a touch screen to select the programs, women will seize the remotes and store them away for the prosperity of future generations.

7. Eyeglasses: Lasik surgery and contacts will rule the vision world. The antique value of all the eyeglasses we've sent to third-world countries will help lift them out of poverty.

8. Twist ties: A twist tie is never more important than when you don't have one. The sheer simplicity of its design makes it collectible or at least worthy of a science-museum display: "Twist Ties through the Ages."

9. Calendars (all kinds—wall, pocket, desk, etc.): Remember how large and expensive the first electronic calculators were? Then they got smaller, became battery-powered, and as inexpensive as a child's toy. I can see the same happening as conventional calendars soar in the antique market, replaced by iCal.

10. Photo albums: Computers will become the family archive—no more anonymous photos jumbled in shoeboxes.

But I still think I'll hang on to those shoeboxes . . .

Home, Sweet Home Remedies

On a rare occasion when I wore a dress to church, I was flattered during the service to see Jack casting an admiring glance at my legs. While I was secretly pleased, I dutifully nudged him to pay attention to the sermon. I later learned he wasn't rhapsodizing over my middle-aged calves, tending toward post-birth varicose veins. He was scrutinizing my nylons for runs.

He had a perfectly good reason—he fills ruined pantyhose with rock salt, knots the open end, and flings them onto the edge of the roof. It's an old home remedy to melt roof ice and try to prevent ice-dam buildup.

Last winter, I pulled into the driveway with our eldest sapling after he had been away at college. When he saw the pregnant tubes of pantyhose adorning the roof, he dubbed it, "The Attack of the Nylons."

I like to think that when the going gets tough here in Minnesota, the tough make do—it can also be called making it up as we go along.

While we're on the topic of stockings and home remedies, it must have been an inventive Lake Country pioneer who first used nail polish to stop a run. I can picture the scenario: It was forty-plus below zero. No doubt it was the actual temperature, well before the days of windchill—it was so cold she considered warning her saplings again about not licking the pump handle.

She was taking a nice pan of bars to a potluck or perhaps a lutefisk dinner. Her last pair of nylons had a run, but she didn't give it a second thought. Due to the cold, she was "layering." Her hosiery-clad legs would be snugly encased inside thermal underwear, which would be covered by warm, sensible corduroy slacks—no one would know her little secret. In her haste to finish her manicure and get to the potluck before the popular green Jell-O salad with carrots was gone, she accidentally dripped nail polish on her stockings and was amazed to see that it stopped the run in its tracks. A new home remedy was born.

Home remedies must have gained most of their popularity in the olden days, before twenty-four-hour shopping was invented. Now when we run out of something, we can go to the store anytime, day or night. Forget looking around the house for something to unclog the drain. Buy a can of Glop-B-Gone. Electric roof de-icer? How long a piece do you want?

But if everything we need can truly be found in the pot of gold at the end of the mall rainbow, and we no longer need home remedies, then why do I have pantyhose adorning my roof? Ask Jack. I guess the old habits—and remedies—die hard.

Wee Jack's Excellent College Adventures

Wee Jack has been begging to go back to college ever since he was three and we paid a weekend visit to Jack, Jr.'s campus. While observing W.J. scamper up and down the lofted beds like a blonde spider monkey, I realized he was three going on thirteen.

After the next event, I didn't know what to think.

We were on our way to drop off Jack, Jr. at the dorm. W.J. was in his car seat in the back seat, beside Junior. Wee Jack leaned over, and casually, conversationally, asked his college-bound brother, "So, do the space ships wake *you* up at night?" He was so matter-of-fact, it sounded like nocturnal visits from little green men were a regular occurrence in his young world and he wanted to know if the same held true for his brother.

Last spring Wee Jack returned to campus, but this time without his parents monitoring his every move. Jack, Jr. invited six-year-old W.J. to Little Sibs (siblings) visitation weekend at his college.

I had several motherly misgivings: What if W.J. couldn't find the bathroom in the middle of the night? Junior was a heavy sleeper and slept on the top bunk. If nature called and W.J. tried to answer, he'd be stumbling around on his own in a strange place. What if he got homesick? What if . . . what if . . . Junior parried every concern with: "It'll be okay, Mom." I finally agreed to entrust my last baby into the tender, loving care of my first baby.

Junior and I met halfway to the Cities at a convenience store to hand off the kid. As I pulled into the parking lot, I felt like a divorced parent sharing custody for the weekend. It wasn't far from the truth—I witnessed the same occurrence with another family in adjacent vehicles. If anyone had been watching us closely, they would have noticed that the main difference in our situation (besides the obvious disparity in our ages!) was when I gave W.J. to Junior, he reciprocated by gifting me with his dirty laundry.

The siblings event kicked off on Friday night with a movie after supper, followed by a trip to the Minnesota Zoo on Saturday. I sent a disposable camera with W.J. so he could take pictures of all the fun he was having.

Junior told me he had already planned to visit a friend's apartment that evening after the siblings' movie, but he said he'd put W.J. to bed at the home around 10:00 p.m.—letting him sleep until Junior was ready to return to campus.

When W.J. came home, I pumped him for information and he gave me another important detail about the evening. "On the way to the house, Junior asked if I wanted to play a trick on some girls," said an animated W.J. "He hid around the corner and I knocked on their door and said, 'I'm lost, do you know where Junior is?'"

W.J. had so much fun playing Nintendo at the apartment that Junior let him play until midnight—four hours after W.J.'s usual bedtime. It was like an extended playdate, only with a captive audience. Junior's friends thought W.J. was the cutest thing since Tickle Me Elmo. (Sidenote: Tickle Me Elmo terrorized W.J. the Christmas it was the Toy of the Season. W.J. couldn't even be coaxed into walking down the toy aisle that contained the hysterical Muppet. Thank goodness Santa and I found out before committing some very serious greenbacks to that gift.)

By the time they returned to campus and W.J. was tucked in under his Sesame Street blanket, it was 2:00 a.m. Wee Jack slept in until 8:00 a.m., which is late for him—he's usually up by six. "It's light outside," he announced to Junior. "It's morning."

"Go back to sleep," muttered Junior. W.J. has never gone back to sleep a day in his life. He was up for the day and ready for the zoo. Missing breakfast allowed W.J. to add to his college experience repertoire by enjoying his first brunch, but he didn't care—the Happy Meal Junior bought him came with a toy car.

Getting to the zoo was almost as much fun as the zoo itself. It was W.J.'s first ride on a schoolbus. Junior almost convinced him that it was a magic, flying school bus, like on TV. W.J. isn't usually that gullible—it must have been due to the sleep deprivation.

After running around the zoo for three hours, W.J. denied he was tired, then promptly fell asleep in Junior's lap on the bus ride back to campus. When I met them at the gas station to reswap the kid, W.J. disembarked clutching his camera, his Happy Meal car, and a bag of candy.

A good time was had by all. I wonder if the spaceships were paying attention?

Memory and Smell

Our olefactory sense is one that evokes deep memories. I have always been able to "smell spring," and until I do, spring isn't really here. Seeing the first robin means nothing if the satisfying aroma of thawing earth doesn't accompany the sighting. And we all know that robins come home too early anyway. I wish I could let them know when it's safe, but then again, I still haven't taken off my snow tires because I don't trust the weather. One year's April 24th blizzard still resonates in my memory bank.

What other smells bring up memories? When our youngest was a baby, I used to tease his big brothers that they can smell him after his bath once for free, but the next whiff would cost a quarter! Who doesn't love the sweet scent of a freshly bathed baby?

Other smells I'm actually looking forward to in a weird way:

* Wet dog, fresh from the lake—it means we've enjoyed a hot, sandy day at the beach.

* Skunk (called "Peppermint Kitty" in our family)—they don't come out till spring either so it's a sure sign of the season.

* Barbeque grill smoke in the air—we grill year round, but the smell of grills warming up in the summer is one to be savored.

* Sunscreen—I love the smell of the "coconutty" one, but sadly, it doesn't come in a high-enough SPF.

* The commingled smells of budding trees, blooming flowers, and rich earth. It can be enjoyed best from the roof, while cleaning out the eaves. Climb the ladder and spend an hour on the roof enjoying the view and the scents of spring.

* Lake—my Arizona sister wants me to figure out a way to bottle the smell of lake.

A Minnesota lake on a spring or summer afternoon will *always* be the best smell in the world.

Summer

~ Sports Talk ~

For years, I've perfected the cheering lingo of the various sports our sapling sons have played. Each one has its own unique language.

* Baseball: Nice cut—Good hit—Right to the glove—Just play catch—Run it out!

* Basketball: Tough D!—Arms up—Look for the ball—Box out—Nice shot.

* Track: Keep it going—Stay strong—Go, go, go!

And now it's tennis. And I'm silenced.

My son quickly pointed out, just in time for his first meet, that shouting for your kid on the tennis court is poor etiquette. I'm required to stand mutely behind the fence, smiling when my son sneaks a glance my way before a serve. It's hard. I've been cheering for my sons for so many years, it's not easy to watch silently.

Being silenced has also given me a new appreciation for the requirements of the sport. I pay closer attention to the forms and styles of the players and watch the boundary lines. But when my husband is at the match (a former tennis champion, himself), I still always, ALWAYS, have to ask him about the scoring.

Scoring aside, these lessons in silence make me more attentive to the nuances of the sport, as well as the nuances of my son.

But in my head, I'm still cheering like crazy.

~ • ~

~ Grown Only Locally ~

I've always been a country mouse. We lived on a lake when I was a child—before the current trend of megabucks luxury lakehomes. It was affordable then. My city-mouse friends thought all country-mice lived on farms. I introduced them to the pleasures of sledding down a country lane with no fear of traffic, ice-skating without waiting for the rink to open (complete with our own private fish house/warming house), and on steamy summer evenings, swimming long after city beaches were closed to the public. I was even too Minnesota Nice to ditch them on a snipe hunt.

Being a young country mouse had two unique milestones. Instead of becoming old enough to cross the street, we were given permission to traipse alone down the shore. Our destination was the mom-and-pop Cast-a-Bait Resort, where we would push our coins across the tall counter to proprietors Slug or Vi to purchase creamy orange Dreamsicles. Mom kept a watchful eye from the living room picture window as we dallied our way down the shore—climbing over docks and looking for agates at the water's edge—we just never knew it.

Our second country living milestone was measuring our height, not just against the usual closet doorframe, but by swimming another dock section deeper as we grew. Countless warnings about the steep drop-off at the end of the dock gained our compliance in not venturing beyond our parent-assigned dock post.

My older sister and I didn't even make our spending money like our city counterparts. A lemonade stand wasn't very profitable when passing cars were few and far between. We sold frogs. (I was surprised to learn later that girls were supposed to be squeamish around frogs—it must be a learned behavior.) Frogs were large and plentiful. Slug and Vi at the resort encouraged our entrepreneurial efforts—their vacationing fishermen were always interested in trying out the local bait. We charged ten cents apiece, or three for a quarter. Since I was small for my age, therefore, less likely to be turned down, I was the one who had to knock on the cabin doors.

We chased frogs along our weedy shoreline, or trapped them in the long grass and bushes growing along the bank, then we quickly stuffed them into shoeboxes with holes punched in the lids. This maneuver required split-second timing—one person to hold the cover open wide enough to squeeze in a frog, the other to quickly stuff it in before the other captives leaped to freedom.

One afternoon, after we'd caught enough to sell, my sister and I were safely ensconced in the enclosed back porch where the frogs couldn't escape. After losing some of our earlier inventory, we'd found they were easier to count if we divided them between a couple of boxes. I told her I had to get something out of the house and went inside. I grabbed our mother's "so-ugly-it's-cute," carved, wooden frog with the yellow-plastic bug-eyes and brought it back in my cupped hands. "We forgot one," I said, and quickly stuck my opened palm in her face. She screamed and dropped the shoebox, which sent frogs leaping for freedom—then she tried to kill me. The only other time I saw her move that fast was when she danced the "There's a moth in the crotch of my still-damp swimsuit off the clothesline" boogie.

Country girls grow up and so do their pastimes. Big Sis traded playing with frogs for a slightly larger animal—a horse. Koko threw her from his back, which gave her a slight concussion, he lost track of his big feet and stepped on our little sister, and he tried to take a bite out of the car's trunk. Dad wondered for years where the mysterious scratches on the car originated.

Granted, Koko made a nifty 4-H project—much more enticing than my presentation on planting radish seeds. How I stretched that into a five-minute demonstration, I'll never know. What is there besides poking your finger into the dirt, dropping in a tiny seed, and covering it up again? Adding water stretches it to thirty-five seconds, tops.

City kids had run-of-the-mill cats, dogs, goldfish, and the occasional hamster. We had muskrats hiding in the tires that hung from the dock posts and kamikaze chipmunks sneaking bits of food from under the semi-watchful eye of our St. Bernard. Try keeping a St. Bernard within city limits.

Granted, city kids learned to roller-skate, but they had an unfair advantage—sidewalks and streetlights. They could walk to the movie theater. We had to beg a ride just to go into town. They also had more friends within a square-block radius. But we had acres—miles if we dared—in which to play Kick the Can or Ditch after dark, under a full moon or canopy of endless stars.

Home, sweet country-mouse home.

(*For Laura)

~ Reunited We Stand ~

"Make new friends, keep the old, one is silver, the other is gold. A circle is round, it has no end, that's how long I'm gonna be your friend."

At my age I've finally achieved the self-confidence necessary to successfully tell little white lies about a few things—minor details ranging from real hair color to financial status. As I contemplate attending my next high-school reunion, I can't imagine feeling comfortable in a whole roomful of people who all know my correct age—not to mention what I really looked like in my high school yearbook picture. When something is "re" anything (remodeled, recycled, retooled), it means finding a new use for an old thing. Attending a reunion doesn't sound very reassuring.

A few years ago I saw an ad in the newspaper for a five-year class get-together. It struck me that five years is much too early to hold a "get-together." They were wise not to call it a class reunion. That would have put them in the category with the rest of us ancients. I think there's a rule that a fairly significant interval of time must pass first. No halfway-decent reunion can take place until the hair recedes and the paunch proceeds.

My favorite kind of reunion takes place purely by happenstance. I am continually surprised at how many classmates still live in our hometown. Where do they hide? Twenty years after a guy was supposed to have relocated to Timbuktu (or at least the suburbs of Hinckley), I see him in the produce department at Cub Foods.

"So, how's it going," I begin, surprised to see him wearing jeans instead of exotic native dress. "How is Timbuktu these days?"

"Oh, I never went after all," supposed-expatriot reveals. "I decided to stick around."

He isn't living in a mud-and-grass shack, toasting snakes over an open firepit, and digging a trench out back for hygiene purposes. He lives in a one-bedroom apartment near the tracks, has a job selling sweaters at the mall, and owns up to having cats—several cats. "My family says I'm two cats short of being crazy people." There isn't much else to talk about. We part company, promising to get together for coffee sometime, and I continue browsing the zucchini selection.

Another type of random reunion occurred one sunny fall afternoon at a women's seminar at a nearby camp. To set the stage, I was never a cheerleader in high school, even though I was often mistaken for one in college. I must have looked perky and capable of completing a round-off without gasping for breath or pulling a hamstring. After registering for the seminar workshops, I turned around and bumped into Katie-Cheerleader from high school. This is not her real name. Even though she has a real last name, she will always be Katie-Cheerleader—hyphenated—in my mind. Why? Even though we graduated into real life, I find we still think in terms of the high-school stereotypes we wore as comfortably (or uncomfortably) as old shirts. Read the following—is there a face/name that instantly pops into your mind?

The Brain
The Artist
The Nerd
The Jock
The Homecoming Queen
The Recluse

I was voted Class Writer. The trouble is everyone expects me to have published the Great American Novel several years ago. Maybe I'll start a rumor it was published under a pen name. I find you can hide a lot behind a great *nom de plume*.

I'll be the first to sign up for my next reunion. My inquiring mind wants to find out why Timbuktu never made it off the continent. I'll ask if Katie-Cheerleader can still do a round-off, and if anyone else found out that our first-grade teacher had a breakdown after our class graduated into second grade. (I swear my antics had nothing to do with it!)

It's tempting to stay home—telling myself it won't be any fun—but then I imagine trying to guess which guy (or girl) lost the most hair, or which girl (or guy) was the first to get a facelift. I'll make a sincere effort to check the high-school stereotypes at the door. I won't assume Gear Head will show up in a Ferrari. We may be all pleasantly surprised to find Radio Club is the millionaire inventor in baggy pants and scruffy hair. And I'd love to find out I have more in common with Class President than I ever did in high school.

Look for me. I'll be the youngest one there, with the natural-looking haircolor.

˜ • ˜

❧ Jackie ❧
The Teen Years

It was the ultimate camping experience—six weeks tent-camping out of a Volkswagen hatchback with my parents and eleven-year-old little sister. I was a month away from turning the sophisticated age of fifteen. We toured the Wild West, with several adventures along the way. The length of our stay in any one place depended on the number of tourist traps/sites. Wall Drug, Mount Rushmore, the Corn Palace, Hoover Dam, Chinatown, Lake Louise, and Lake Vegas, to name a few.

My mother was the consummate packer—in a VW, you had to be. There was a place for everything. I had to bring a hat. I'm not sure why I loathed hats, unless it was because my mother knew what was good for my fair skin and I didn't want to admit she was right. I was a teenager, after all. My hat had a big, floppy brim and was a green/brown/gold floral print. I remember starting out with a hat, but I'm quite sure I ditched it somewhere in the Black Hills, probably corresponding to my black mood at the time.

After reaching the campground and helping set up the tent, we girls were free to explore. This was the late sixties, when parents didn't need to worry that their daughters would be kidnapped and carried across state lines for nefarious purposes.

At a campground somewhere in the Rocky Mountains, I met a runaway teenage boy on his way to California to pursue freedom from parental restraints. I felt cool—wearing my best bell-bottom jeans with white stars I'd sewn on myself—and slightly conspiratorial as I talked to this strange breed of one of my peers. The boys I knew back home were safely involved in 4-H, summer jobs, and baseball. This one was a hippie—or at least a hippie wannabe. I promised not to turn him in, and I definitely didn't mention the conversation to my parents. I occasionally wonder if he ever found happiness.

Along the way, besides camping, our family stayed briefly in motels to clean up—sleeping and showering in comfort. We even visited an aunt and uncle in sunny California. They took us out for dinner at Farrell's Ice Cream Parlour where—if the establishment learned it was your birthday—you were forced to stand on a chair while they served your treat and everyone sang "Happy Birthday." Even though my birthday was two weeks away, my uncle teased me unmercifully, and I lived in mortal teenage fear that my secret would be leaked before we got out of Dodge.

We spent a couple of nights in Las Vegas. I was amazed by the city that never sleeps—walking through the lobby on the way to breakfast I saw people gambling who hadn't gone to bed the night before. Clutching cups of coins, they interrupted their rhythmic slot-machine choreography only long enough to take pulls from cups of lukewarm coffee, or a watered-down, complimentary highball.

The outdoor swimming pool was awe-inspiring to a small-town girl. Not the run-of-the-mill rectangular model, it was lushly landscaped and surrounded with lounge chairs beckoning my sister and me to stretch out and work on our tans. I was proud of my bright-orange velour one-piece swimming suit with its cut-outs attached with white plastic rings.

I decided to test the water and descended the steps into the pool. As the water reached my waist—to my complete and utter horror—I watched as the iodine-based pool chemicals turned my orange suit an ugly brown. I raced back to the hotel room, my sister close at my heels. All Mom could recommend was submerging my entire body so I wouldn't have a half-orange, half-brown suit. I tearfully complied—with my sister also appearing to mourn the demise of my orange coolness.

Deciding my sister and I needed cheering up, I took my newfound Las Vegas sophistication a step further and ordered two Cokes from the strolling poolside waitress. After a long wait, she returned with the tall, frosty drinks, each embellished with cute umbrellas and two fancy, skinny straws. I hadn't asked the price and thought they would cost the same as a Coke at Scott's lunch counter back home. I was mortified—as only a teenager can be—to find I didn't have enough money. The kind waitress covered the missing amount for me. I think she paid the balance out of her tips. From the scanty uniform she was wearing, I think her tips were probably more than enough to cover the shortage.

Could poolside events get any worse? Of course they could. Sis and I commandeered two pool mattresses to float in the sparkling blue water. As we comfortably paddled around, a woman came to tell us that those were the mattresses she'd rented for her children and we had to return them to the poolside. Rented? I thought they were free. Shame-faced for the third time in one afternoon, we returned to the room.

I've never returned to Las Vegas. I don't think I ever recovered from the overwhelming angst it caused my inner teenager. I now have a deeper appreciation for the tranquilities of a Minnesota summer: a clear, blue lake, a reasonably priced can of pop, and an oversized, black innertube—such simple joys are priceless.

❧ Born to Be Wild ❧

We live in the Land of 10,000 Lakes—vacation Mecca for thousands. But for some reason, our family doesn't think we're having a real vacation unless it takes us several hours to reach our location. I use the term *vacation* rather loosely. Other people take vacations; we seem to get *learning experiences*.

Every summer, Jack, the saplings, and I head off in one direction or another. If I would ever remember to pack the video camera, we could easily produce a sequel of *Chevy Chase Vacation*. Take, for example, the year we went out to the Black Hills.

The South Dakota border has a really nice, well-lit rest stop with a large road map next to the sidewalk. As I traced our route on the map, I was vaguely aware of what sounded like a flock of birds in the tree a few feet from the map—and a very few feet from where I was standing. Just then Jack said, "Look at all the bats!"

A flock? swarm? gaggle? A BUNCH of bats had taken over the tree and were swooping back and forth, gabbling at each other. Be forewarned: In South Dakota after dark, bats meet you at the border.

We jumped in the van, Jack drove, and I began looking for a town large enough to have a motel. I teased the kids that if we didn't find a nice motel, we were going to stay in a dive. We believe in expanding our children's vocabulary at every opportunity. We'd also been seeing quite a few motorcycles.

"That's right," Jack remarked offhandedly. "I heard on the news that it's around the time for the Sturgis Motorcycle Rally." I grabbed the map and was relieved to find that we wouldn't pass anywhere near Sturgis.

By now, it was 10:00 p.m. and a few smaller towns we went through had No Vacancy signs lit over their motels. We decided our best bet would be Sioux Falls. But the far-reaching impact of Sturgis was worse than we imagined. Motel after motel blazed No Vacancy and the parking lots were crammed with motorcycles. With a sinking feeling, we realized that, on the interstate across South Dakota, there was no room at the inn.

Jack looked at me across the dimly lit dashboard and said, "I guess we go all night." I shivered with the excitement that can only come from adrenaline and caffeine.

We pulled into a truck stop and filled the thermos with more black coffee. Then I heard myself say perkily, "I'll take the first shift." I'm the into-my-jammies-and-early-to-bed type. I thought I'd drive for maybe an hour or two, then turn it back over to Jack and get some sleep. So he poured my coffee, I set the cruise control (love those interstate speeds!), and we hit the road.

At 5:30 the next morning, I pulled over and let Jack pilot us into Rapid City. Eating at a truck stop next to a big table of folks in black leather, boots, and in need of a hot shower, lent new meaning to the phrase, "Kids, it is not polite to stare." You understand, as in "I don't want to meet these nice people out in the parking lot later."

We spent a few minutes at Mt. Rushmore, realized that it hadn't changed in the four years since our last visit, and moved on to Jewel Cave. After an awesome tour, our guide told us to ask her about road construction detours.

Jack checked it out. "Guess what? We have to backtrack." Backtracking put us ten miles from the epicenter of the Sturgis Motorcycle Rally.

Have you seen the bumper sticker, "Start Seeing Motorcycles"? We had no trouble seeing motorcycles. We thought there should be a bumper sticker, "Start Seeing Cars."

We saw big Harley choppers with the front fork pitched forward, three-wheel trikes, and big-bucks Honda Gold Wings loaded to the max with all the bells and whistles.

"I've heard that all types come to this thing," Jack mused. "That long-haired, bearded guy could be a doctor, or lawyer—even a dentist." I think I spotted the dentist. He had his chains fastened at the ends with little alligator clips, robbed from his napkin bib stash at work.

It was like being dropped into the middle of a three-ring motorcycle circus. One day we'd look back and laugh. Right now, we had our hands full navigating the twisting, turning mountain roads hemmed in by hordes of motorcycles.

We eventually made it safely past Sturgis. But I'm still experiencing a few lingering aftershocks. Now when passing the local Harley shop, I can't resist taking a second glance—or I find myself wistfully fingering the black leather jacket that turns up at the thrift shop, and my jewelry box reveals a definite trend toward chains.

But the worst one is my recurring dream of parking my suburban mini-van at Wal-Mart, climbing onto a "hog" and gluing myself tightly to Jack's back, and riding off into the sunset with the summer breeze warm on my face.

P.S. I almost forgot to tell you what we learned. We figured out how to take a trip to South Dakota without being tempted into Wall Drug—just cruise on by at 3:00 a.m.

Not Bonkers over Beanies

Warning: *Due to the graphic nature of the Beanie Baby handling referred to in this essay, bona fide Beanie collectors may want to skip it altogether and proceed to the next entry.*

As a schoolchild, I loved playing beanbag relay games in gym class. I loved the feel of the beans in the beanbag shifting from end to end within its thin, cotton casing. The smooth, rhythmic *chkkk-chkkk-chkkk* of the beans calmed me before my turn to run.

A few years ago, the lowly beanbag had been elevated from its earlier status of something to be tossed across a dusty gym floor, to pricey TY Beanie Babies being pitched into the cacophony of clamoring collectors. The Beanie Babies rise to fame was similar to a Little League player going from the neighborhood sandlot to commanding mega-millions at the Metrodome. At one time, a McDonald's Teeny Beanies Happy Meal bag alone was worth six dollars in some cities. Just.The.Bag. I wondered if the grease spots increased or decreased the value?

I never did understand the logic surrounding the Beanie craze. For years, stuffed toys had come with warning labels urging the purchasers to "remove all tags before giving the toy to children." But Beanie Babies with dangling tags were clutched by sticky-fingered children—if the kids were lucky enough to first pry them loose from the tight fists of their collector parents.

Even spin-off Beanie merchandising was lost on me. Beanie clothes, houses, display cases, and—my personal favorite—tag protectors. I would never purchase a tag protector. In my household, I'd need a protector to protect the protector. We were never as bad as Sid, the evil toy-torturer, in *Toy Story*. Our abuses were minor—to all but a Beanie collector.

We treated Beanies as—toys. Wee Jack played with them. When he was three years old that usually involved a rambunctious game of Catch or Keep Away across the family room. He especially loved the sound Beanies made when they were caught, and then ripped from, a Velcro catcher's mitt. The tags never lasted long.

I once read that the TY folks wanted to get more Beanies into the hands of children. The way we treated their product, the TY people should have been pleased. I'm just afraid that, if I stumbled upon a $425 Libearty the Bear for two bucks at a garage sale, I might be tempted to reform my errant Beanie-havior.

North Woods Wanna-Beanies:
1. Vermin the Muskrat
2. Sneaky the Weasel
3. Creepy-crawly the Woodtick
4. Chug-a-lug the Mosquito
5. Babe the Blue Ox
6. Daddy the Long Legs
7. Loony the Loon
8. Greedy the Gull
9. Cagey the Snipe
10. Slimy the Eelpout

Will the Real Mrs. Minnesota...

In a rare opportunity to channel surf (rare because Jack didn't control the remote—he must have been out-of-town), I came across the Mrs. Minnesota pageant. Many little girls dream of becoming Miss America. I've been disqualified due to my marital status, so I found myself watching these married contestants, wondering if I'd have the chutzpah to compete. But as I watched, I thought of the Velveteen Rabbit. He became real only after he had been loved so much by his little boy owner that his fur was rubbed off. I wanted to see those coiffed, made-up, sequined, sparkled, and Spandexed wives and mothers looking—real.

For example, there's the fitness portion of the contest. To prove they were physically fit, they had to don dancewear, learn a routine, and perform flawlessly in front of a live audience, with thousands more watching on television. How many Mrs. enjoy parading around the YMCA locker room in exercise garb, let alone in front of complete strangers analyzing their body mass and dexterity? I identified with one motherly type, placed unobtrusively in the back row. I, too, could never match kicks with the few aerobic Barbies who appeared to have been poured into their costumes.

The physical fitness of Mrs. Minnesota should be measured by her ability to maintain her equilibrium while simultaneously taking a hot cookie sheet out of the oven, balancing a screaming toddler on one hip, and talking on the telephone. Or, at the very least, her stamina following an all-nighter spent rocking/cleaning up after a child suffering from the vomit/diarrhea flu and, come morning, realizing it's her turn to drive the carpool for her other children. She should sport a low-maintenance, shower-to-chauffeur hairdo, love handles unadorned by Spandex, and wrinkles of experience that haven't been nipped and tucked into oblivion.

Which brings me to another category: talent. If a contestant has memorized Beethoven's *Fifth* and can play it on a panpipe, let her go on a concert tour. But I think the qualities needed to make it as a Minnesota wife/mother would be more adequately measured by one of the following:

1. Juggling: Four separate sport/music lesson/play date schedules, while not missing an event or losing/forgetting a child.

2. Choreography: The intricate dance of keeping your home clean enough not to be condemned yet still fool your friends by its resemblance to Martha Stewart's.

3. Speaking: When told that your sixteen-year-old just wrecked the new minivan, murmuring wise words about life's lessons as you calmly dial the insurance agency—instead of screaming, tearing out someone's hair, or kicking the dog.

4. Racing: To the house with a wheelbarrow load of firewood before the embers in the stove die out.

5. Dressing: A toddler in snowsuit, boots, hat, mittens, and muffler—then learning that he has to "go potty"—and *patiently* repeating the process in reverse.

6. Singing: The praises of family values while society tries to rewrite your job description.

A couple of other categories could use some minor revisions, too. Instead of modeling evening gowns, I think we'd be more comfortable sporting flannel nightgowns. Sew on a few sequins and we'd fit right in. Or take the interview question—let's leave world affairs to the politicians—I'd want to know what they'd say if their teenager came in after curfew sporting a colorful tattoo and draped with his new girlfriend.

And finally, the escorts. Are those gorgeous hunks in tuxedos really their husbands? And if so, how would I ever corral/shanghai/hogtie Jack into doing that for me? Getting him into the tux would be hard enough, not to mention escorting me across a stage in front of hundreds of people, plus aforementioned television audience. The men were even asked a spontaneous question by the emcee. They all had such cute, scripted answers, they must have been forewarned to prepare an off-the-cuff response.

What if I won? We'd both be required to make guest appearances at future Mrs. Minnesota contests well into the next century. Can you imagine the pressure not to let yourself go blissfully into middle-age spread? The frantic dieting and exercising preceding each year's pageant? The only way out would be to volunteer for a spot on the next space mission—annually. The stress factor on a marriage would rank with planning a wedding, childbirth, root canal, and an IRS audit—all in one year.

Let's have a real Midwestern pageant. Any suggestions on how to trick Jack into escorting me?

✧ Souvenirs of Summer ✧

Souvenirs come in many shapes and sizes. We stuff our closets with clothing ("My kids bicycled to Hack-n-back and all I got was this lousy T-shirt."), store musty boxes with shells we collected on beaches at a seaside paradise, or display dusty, miniature birchbark canoes—stamped "Made in Sri Lanka"—that are guaranteed to be assembled with bark harvested from deadfall trees.

What happens when we go on vacation? We spend money for items we would never give a second glance if we were at home. There must be a mutant gene that kicks in when we cross the county line. It dispenses a hormone that releases the mechanism that usually keeps our fingers clutched in a death grip on our wallets. Over many years of taking family vacations, I've decided that souvenirs fall into two categories: some cost nearly nothing yet leave lasting memories, while some cost big bucks *and* make great memories.

When Jack and I were newlyweds, our first vacation together was a camping/fishing expedition. We brought along all our own food, so our only purchases were a cheap, orange plastic raincoat, fishing licenses, and fresh bait. Our souvenirs were the memory of battling the waves in our canoe when a sudden squall came up on the lake, and a large piece of driftwood we brought home to decorate our yard. At the border, when we told the customs official that we had nothing to declare except the raincoat, his look of disbelief led me to fear he would divert our van to the side of the road and give it the customs equivalent of a vehicle strip search.

Another time, we attended a family reunion in the Tetons. With two young children, I had a hard time justifying spending vacation money on myself. We had to budget our food, gas, camping, and souvenir money carefully over the full two weeks. One week into the trip, I found myself in a clothing store, browsing the selection of ladies' sweatshirts. I have expensive taste—the sweatshirt I liked cost thirty-five dollars. I realize that on the Sweatshirt Scale of Economics, thirty-five dollars doesn't sound like much. But since you've been reading *Northern Comfort*, you know that I have a hard time:

A) Spending money on myself when the kids might need it. It's called the Mother Martyr Syndrome—the premise on which it is based is fodder for countless stories.

B) Paying full retail when I can find a great buy on the ever-present clearance rack.

I knew that once I bought the sweatshirt, one of the children would immediately find a perfect souvenir they absolutely couldn't live without, and my ensuing motherly guilt would cause me to cringe—caught redhanded—within the pricey sweatshirt on my back.

I bought the sweatshirt and never regretted it. In fact, every time I put it on or even see it in my drawer, I'm reminded of the great time our family spent together and I get that warm-fuzzy vacation glow all over again.

In the great memories/big bucks category, is a boat propeller . . .

We were on a fishing trip with our young sons on Lake of the Woods, notorious for its underwater rock formations. Jack had just returned from a morning fishing/scouting expedition, and picked us up in the boat to go for a ride. He chose to show us a part of the lake we hadn't seen before. As we cruised along, I asked Jack if there were any rocks in the area.

"No, I was just here this morning," he said, consulting the map, "they're farther in towards shore." Just then we heard a sickening crunch and the boat jerked to a halt. Envisioning water spouting from a gaping hole in the hull, I made sure the boys' life jackets were strapped on tightly. We paddled the boat, blessedly intact, toward shore—leaving several, good-sized chunks of our propeller decorating the lakebed.

The bad news? We totalled the prop. The good news? Jack (Eagle Scout graduate and the one I'd want on my team during a zombie apocalypse) had brought along a spare. While he labored to replace the prop, the boys and I watched from the shore. Then I noticed several turkey vultures perched in the trees. Remember the desert scenes in the movies? When the hungry vultures first circle and then perch, waiting for the hapless wanderers to succumb to the elements? I kept a close eye on the boys, tightened the rope that secured the boat to shore, and quickly helped everyone aboard when the repair was complete.

When we returned home, we kept the damaged prop. It makes a nice doorstop—and a great visual when we share our vacation stories with others.

Cherish your own vacation souvenirs and remember—summer's too short—spring for the sweatshirt.

~ And the Survey Says! ~

June is traditionally "wedding month," but in 1977, Jack and I got married in April. April in Minnesota is much like February, only with robins shivering in skimpy, red-breasted jackets. I chose a heavy satin gown with long sleeves, which normally would have been suitable attire for a cooler, early spring wedding. However, in 1977, the temperature on our wedding day hit eighty-six degrees. Jack and I have been breaking records ever since.

Jack was twenty-five when we met. Yes, an older man. Since he had already waited that long, he decided he wouldn't get married until he was thirty, like his Uncle Jim did. Six days into our honeymoon, we celebrated Jack's twenty-sixth birthday.

Deciding when to get married is only half the battle of surviving thirty-seven years of wedded bliss. Blending family traditions also took a little getting used to. Does the toilet paper roll from the top or the bottom? Are long-needled Christmas trees superior to short-needled ones? Do we open gifts on Christmas Eve or Christmas Day? What holidays do we spend with which set of in-laws? (That one was decided for us when my parents relocated to the hinterlands of the Wild, Wild West.)

Even holiday food brings its own set of questions. On Christmas Eve, my family ate Danish *ebleskiver* (a ball-shaped pancake stuffed with fruit). Jack's traditional food was oyster stew. Thankfully, the oyster stew tradition is devolving its way to extinction as the grown cousins opt for a new tradition—wild rice soup.

Who gets which side of the bed? Do we get up as soon as the alarm clock goes off or hit the snooze button for half an hour? And who is in charge of said snooze button? Who lets the dogs out at night? Who makes the coffee in the morning while letting the dogs out again? What kind of meal shall we have on Sunday night? That one turned out to be more complicated than it might sound.

My mother put three square meals on the table seven days a week, but she took a well-deserved evening off on Sundays. Every man/woman/child fended for him/herself—leftovers, cereal, toast and jam—whatever could be scrounged before the siblings nabbed it. On one of Jack's and my first Sunday evenings, I went into the kitchen to rustle myself some grub. Jack moseyed along behind. I was shoulders-deep in the cupboard when he made his presence known.

"What's for supper?" he asked.

"I don't know about you," I replied nonchalantly, "but I'm having graham crackers and milk." His openmouthed stare has since reached epic proportions as a classic Jack Savage moment.

I also discovered early on—before the terminology had been developed to describe the phenomenon—that Jack is severely "mall-challenged." Shortly after it opened, we took our saplings to the Mall of America. Even though we started our venture in a sports store, it was too much for Jack. Thirty minutes later, he headed for a motel shuttle bus—and it wasn't even the bus for our motel. It's a good thing I know his sizes and pick up things for him on my mall errands or his Jockeys would be extremely threadbare by now. He has been MOA-averse ever since.

I recently saw an ad for a *Wedding Kit for Dummies* book. I think a *Marriage Kit for Dummies* book would have a far-greater impact. We filled out something called a "Marriage Role Expectation Inventory" survey that had been published in 1960. (I'm still trying to figure out why nothing more current had come along by 1977.) We had to choose one of five answers—Strongly Agree, Agree, Undecided, Disagree, or Strongly Disagree—for hypothetical marriage questions.

I found our surveys the other day. I laughed so hard I cried. Jack answered "Strongly Disagree" to the question: "In my marriage I expect to leave the care of the children entirely up to my wife when they are babies." I can count on half of one hand the number of diapers he changed. If I left the wee saplings with Daddy-dearest, I left a detailed list to guarantee their survival until my return. When our first sapling was born, I made a run to the grocery store. Jack sent his work pager along in case of an "emergency." I almost made it home within an hour before it went off. I quickly pulled into a store on the highway to use a payphone (this was in the Dark Ages before cellphones). The emergency? The sapling was in urgent need of a diaper change and Jack wanted to know if I'd be home soon.

I asked Jack why the answers on his survey didn't line up with reality. He said he had just put down what he thought I wanted to hear. Amazing. But we made it for thirty-seven years anyway.

❧ • ❧

~ Fair Play ~

I bought cotton candy at a grocery store last winter. It was a squashed bag of colored, limp floss that bore little resemblance to the cones of pure whipped sugar I inhaled at the county fair when I was young. It's a good thing cotton candy wasn't available year round back then. I might have settled for the poor imitation and really rotted my teeth, rather than waiting all year for the delectable spun ambrosia that was only available on the midway.

One year I was in kid heaven. My dad's Kiwanis club opened a cotton candy concession on the fairgrounds. Finally, all the cotton candy my allowance could buy. We had to pay for it like everyone else, but it was the impeccable source that appealed to my family's hygiene sensibilities. Eating cotton candy sold by the carnies seemed to carry a certain amount of risk. It was tasty, we just weren't sure how often they washed their hands after handling all that sweaty money.

Another favorite attraction at the fair were the livestock barns. My sister entered Koko, her quarter-horse gelding, as her 4-H project one year. We didn't have a horse trailer, so she mapped out all the back roads and rode him to the fairgrounds. I think she should have won an endurance ribbon just for riding twenty-five miles one way. Some of the kids camped out in the barns all week, bedding down with their horses, sheep, or cows—inhaling straw dust, animal musk, and carnival excitement twenty-four hours a day.

My little sister was once butted by a mean billy goat at a campground riding stable. Ever since then, Mom exposed us to livestock in non-threatening environments like the fair. The kiddy barn hadn't been invented yet, and even behind sturdy two-by-four fenced enclosures some of the fat sows looked pretty threatening. Gilbertson's stallion kicked at the walls of his enclosed box stall, which caused us to detour in case he bolted for freedom about the time we ambled by. Either he didn't appreciate confinement or he smelled competition and wasn't about to let the other studs get cozy with his harem.

After touring the fair buildings, we grabbed a bite to eat at a church food concession. The grandmas and aunts who did the cooking and serving there were considered trustworthy enough to practice proper hygiene.

Even though we were too small for the wilder rides at the fair, we still saved the best for last—The Midway.

To get to the merry-go-round or the ferris wheel, we had to pass the carnival games. I learned early not to look at the carnies who ran the games. I believed, once they made eye contact, they could talk any passerby out of his hard-earned money without the target customer even being aware it was happening. How else did people take home huge pink teddy bears, when all I ever witnessed someone win was a plastic duck or a flimsy paper blowout whistle? And to this small-town girl, the nomadic life led by the carnies hinted of unknown dangers—tawdry gypsy transience in a teardown, gone-by-morning existence.

I had less of a chance than most at winning the teddy bear, for despite the best efforts of my gym teachers, I still threw like a girl. I'm convinced it's the fault of those horrid one-piece, blue-cotton gymsuits we had to wear. They hung down to our knees and didn't resemble anything a real athlete would wear. It's true. One thing I later learned from theater is the costume makes all the difference.

Not all carnival games involved skill, but even Guess Your Weight is now obsolete. There must not be any money in guessing someone's capacity for concealing their fondness for "ruffles with ridges." I unwittingly played Guess Your Weight as an adult when touring a noisy factory. I inadvertently found myself standing on an in-floor scale. Before I realized it, my weight was displayed on a digital readout for all to see. I still claim my seventeen-pound purse was the culprit.

Now that I'm an adult and can ride the Wild Thing or Tilt-a-Whirl to my heart's content, all my queasy stomach can handle are still the ferris wheel and the merry-go-round. Once when I tried to board a merry-go-round with a sleeping infant strapped to my chest in a carrier, the ride attendant insisted I pay for the baby. Seriously? I handed the baby off to Auntie so I could ride along with the toddlers. Even now, I don't consider the merry-go-round a kiddie ride. I spent many an idyllic afternoon riding carousel steeds with our wee saplings—holding them in place while vicariously enjoying the trip.

Do you remember the one-seat "ferris wheel" ride on the sidewalk outside the Super Valu grocery store years ago? Like store-bought cotton candy, it couldn't take the place of the real thing either. Even now, when I drive onto the county fairgrounds, the sight of the towering ferris wheel spinning its lazy circles in the air makes my heart beat a little bit faster. And the smell of real cotton candy is pure delight, no matter who makes it.

The Babysitter

(Beneath that mild-mannered exterior lurks: The Babysitter.)

Think back to your summer jobs as a young teenager. How many of you babysat? Here are a few of my horror stories:

1) The two-year-old who screamed at the top of his lungs the entire time his parents golfed. I was sitting for them every morning, all week long, at a resort. He never stopped screaming. On Friday, my last day, I had to walk home afterward because no one from the resort could drive me. It was mid-summer, hot, buggy, and a long, dusty, dirt road measured in miles, not blocks. However, since the parents were on vacation, at least they paid well.

2) The parents who came home at 2:00 a.m. (they were supposed to be home at midnight) and reeked of alcohol. My mom and dad weren't very happy when I called saying I would be home late. My dad picked me up and drove me home. They tried to hire me again, but I was always conveniently unavailable, even though they paid well.

3) The time a blizzard knocked out the electricity and I was sitting in a very large house with four sleeping kids, no power,

and no flashlights. I sat next to the phone and called information every few minutes to get the time and hear a friendly voice. I was given a ride home on their snowmobile because the car couldn't make it up the driveway. I believe I got extra hazardous-duty pay that night.

4) The same family in the summer—only with a few extra kids due to a blended family situation. Six kids under the age of twelve versus me—two of them boys who knew how to make killer rubber band guns from wooden rulers. I was unable to bust the rubber band perps until just before the parents got home. I was so frustrated by that time, I snapped the homemade weapons into several pieces. I kept going back because they paid well.

The common denominator of these most-trying babysitting jobs? They all paid well. It must have been a fair trade-off in the mind of a money-hungry teenager with no marketable job skills.

~ Serendipity ~

Serendipity: ". . . finding valuable or agreeable things not sought for" (Webster's Dictionary)

A truly serendipitous event doesn't come along every day.

I've always loved shopping for school supplies. Since I'm now an adult I need to call them "office supplies," but the principle is the same. Even now, back-so-school season infuses me with the nostalgia of new shoes, new notebooks, and finding the perfect box of crayons.

A while ago, I asked my Facebook friends if anyone remembered the "Nifty"—a binder with two holes at the top for special Nifty loose-leaf paper and a magnetic-closure compartment to hold a pencil and eraser. It was from the mid-1960s, so that gives you a clue as to my age.

My Nifty was brown—boring, serviceable brown. Keep in mind, this was before they began marketing colors and designs that would appeal to children. I don't remember how I learned about the Nifty, but every elementary-aged child who was anybody had to have one.

A few days after posing the Nifty question on Facebook, I was on my way home from the flea market and randomly stopped at a garage sale. There wasn't much in the sale assortment that appealed to me and I was about to leave, when I skimmed the last table. There, atop a pile of assorted office supplies, was a distinctive black binder with the "hinge" at the top. Could it be?

Yes. It was a Nifty—fully loaded with the special top-punched paper.

Serendipity strikes again.

Fall

❦ The Numbers Game ❦

I'm so math-challenged, I flunked my Apgar score when I was born. It's not my fault—I arrived a month early and didn't have time to cram. I barely tipped the scales at five pounds. My mother had planned to name me "September," but when I came prematurely, thank goodness she knew "August" wasn't an acceptable girl's name.

I was cheated out of the one-room school experience. The country schoolhouse held first through sixth grades, so I skipped kindergarten. The year I was to begin first grade, we were herded together and shipped to the city on schoolbuses. For the first time, I was cooped up in a desk and not allowed to talk to the new friends seated all around me.

My report card was continually marked: "Needs to refrain from disturbing others." But I guess I wasn't the only one who was having a rough year. Years later, at my twentieth-class reunion, I learned that my first-grade teacher suffered a nervous breakdown the summer after my class graduated to second grade. To this day, I maintain it wasn't entirely my fault.

My education truly began in second grade—we learned to read. But one day I was tricked into swearing by a naughty town boy. He printed a word on a piece of wide-lined paper and taunted that I couldn't read it phonetically.

"That's easy," I said and quickly complied. The boy told the teacher that I swore and I went home crying with a note to give my parents. I didn't know about bad words. Mom and Dad didn't swear—good grief, my role model was Captain Kangaroo! Fortunately, my parents knew the truth and cleared my good name.

In junior high in seventh-grade, I couldn't remember the seat I was assigned in math class. Changing classrooms all day and just getting my locker open had been tricky enough. When I asked for help, the teacher stared at me, not speaking. Shame-faced, I waited along with a few others, and we finally seated ourselves by the process of elimination. I ended up getting sick that winter, fell behind in math, and struggled ever since.

So in twelfth grade, I discovered a loophole that allowed me to drop math to take my beloved creative writing. When I told my math teacher, she said, "Your parents will be so disappointed." Since my father was on the school board, the teachers expected me to excel in all areas of academia. Barely concealing my glee, I said that my parents had already given me their blessing.

Life is funny—my oldest son is now a math teacher. But I'm sure it's only because I never helped him with his homework.

Branching Out

Once, while taking an early-morning walk in my neighborhood, I heard a bird singing in the trees overhead. As a young girl, I grew up with a binoculars on the windowsill and a bird book close at hand. I wanted to identify the source of the birdsong, so my eyes were drawn to the treetops. But instead of focusing on the colorful plumage of a north woods bird, I saw a tree. This was my usual walking route and I had passed this same tree hundreds, if not thousands, of times. For some reason I truly noticed it.

Before I describe the tree and you think I've taken leave of my senses, know I'd not been drinking anything stronger than black coffee. This tree was notable because the bottom trunk half appeared to be an oak and the top half looked like a birch.

I tried to find out that could have happened. One forester theorized that oak sprouts came up through a birch cluster and they grew together. It was later determined it was diseased, thus causing the anomaly. Regardless of how it occurred, my morning walk hasn't been the same since. I have mulled this over and applied it to several different life lessons. The most significant at the time was our son graduating from college to become a math teacher. He definitely didn't get his math genes from me!

How often do we ask children, "What do you want to be when you grow up?" When this son was young, his answer was usually, "An astronaut." We have buckets of space Legos to prove it. As a mother, I'm thankful he gravitated toward an earthbound pursuit. But even when he was preparing to graduate from high school, he still didn't plan on becoming a teacher. A career course he took in high school had directed his math interest into the private sector, so he enrolled in engineering college. A year later, after working with kids as a summer Christian camp counselor, he realized that his heart's desire was to use his math abilities to teach kids.

We don't need to plan our whole lives from start to finish. Be prepared to take a new path, branch out into new discoveries . . . try a different direction.

I know I'm still trying to figure out what I'll be when I grow up.

The Job Description

After Wee Jack's recent playdate at a friend's house (I'll call him Wee John), I received an e-mail from Wee John's mother with a photo attachment. She titled it: "Blackmail." I anxiously waited for it to download. When the photo finally appeared, it revealed Wee Jack and his sidekick wearing cartoon-character underwear on their heads, pretending to be action heroes. Yes, the underwear was clean. I was grateful Wee John's mother had the foresight to snap a picture and indebted for life that she sent it to me.

I am shamefully low on ammunition—those incriminating pictures mothers pull out years later in retaliation for all the trouble their kids put them through. As a mother, keeping such records is in my job description. Wee Jack is our third child and we know baby books become pretty barren farther down the sibling ladder. When Wee Jack was an infant, I had even neglected to pose him bare-bottomed on a bearskin rug—the classic photo to pull out to show the date when Teen Jack finally brings home a girl.

Mothers not only bring home the venison bacon and fry it up in the cast-iron pan—they also maintain the family archives—keeping a top-secret file of embarrassing photos for individual family members. It's even rumored that somewhere there is rare, home-movie footage of a younger Big Jack Savage tapdancing—something he wouldn't want his coffee group to find out.

I've never seen a copy of a mother's job description. I just know what it covers—a lot. Most days I have so many pots on my back burner, it's a miracle they don't boil over. Before allowing herself a nervous breakdown, any mother in her right mind would fill the freezer with dinners, fold and put away the laundry, and take the dog in for shots whether it needed them or not.

We must also archive the wise words spouted by our progeny. These two are keepers from my "Best of the Best" file.

• When taking the oldest sapling to summer camp, I reminded him several times to get his raincoat out of the trunk when we got there. As we pulled into the parking lot, I asked, "What are you going to do now?" "Kiss you quick, while no one's looking?" (Exactly what a weepy mother needs to hear when she's leaving her baby with total strangers for a week.)

• Wee Jack, proudly wearing his brand-new mud boots, was equally eloquent circumnavigating the minefield in the area of the dog's chain after winter's meltdown, prior to spring clean-up. "Don't step in the poop," I cautioned. (You have to spell it out for toddlers.) He replied, "Can I when I'm wearing my poop boots?"

What isn't included in the job description? Time alone.

I discovered the secret behind Mona Lisa's beatific smile when I was meeting a friend for lunch. Wee Jack stayed home with Dad. I arrived early and quietly strolled through the downtown antique shops. Entering the café, I glimpsed my face in the window. I wore a Mona Lisa smile.

During another rare solo moment, I reveled in a solitary picnic in my parked car at the baseball field before our middle sapling's game. I dined sumptuously on a forgotten, cellophane-wrapped package of saltines and half a can of warm Pepsi—pure ambrosia. Had anyone been watching, they would have witnessed the Mona Lisa smile. The truth is, the first Divine Miss M left her tots at home while sitting for the portrait. Posing in silence for hours doesn't sound like a vacation—unless you're a mother.

Then there are the benefits.

When we took our eldest sapling off to college, despite making a list and checking it twice, I still felt like we were forgetting something important. We picked up snacks and a white board for messages—but I still felt there was more I needed to do for my firstborn.

Only after the last "good-bye," did he remember he needed new reeds for his saxophone. It was too late. The stores weren't open and it was almost time for freshman orientation. Jack and I drove through the downtown to pick up coffee before heading home. We passed the music store.

"Let me out, I want to make sure they're closed," I said impulsively. I hopped out and peeked in the window—there was a light on in back, but the showroom was dark. Could they be preparing to open? I tried the doorknob—it turned.

"Are you open?" I called.

"No," came a voice.

"Would it be too much trouble to sell me a couple of reeds?"

"No problem," the owner replied. "I'm not usually here this early, but I stopped in for a minute." The transaction completed, I jumped back in the van. We returned to campus and gave our son the reeds.

I was finally ready to leave. It was time to let him add his harmony to the music of the world.

Letting him go is also in the job description.

⌘ Let's Talk Turkey ⌘
Leftovers: Bane or Blessing?

It's the day after Thanksgiving and most of the nation's cooks are browsing through cookbooks for something new and different to do with twenty-four pounds of leftover turkey, stuffing, and assorted trimmings. Face it—turkey is turkey, no matter how you disguise it, sort of like venison. A friend told me you could marinate venison in gasoline and it would still taste like venison—don't try this at home.

We wouldn't have a problem with leftovers in the first place if it were easier to calculate how many pounds of turkey it takes to feed twenty-five people of various shapes, ages, and appetites. There must be a mathematical equation similar to the one used when matching the ratio of pasta to sauce for spaghetti. Gourmet cooks use a measuring tool for pasta—the correct amount of raw pasta fits into different-sized holes in a small piece of plastic. Imagine the size of the utensil needed to measure the girth of a turkey!

Years ago, my parents had discovered a simple solution. Dad used to fire up the Weber and grill steaks. Steak? For Thanksgiving? Why not? Have you ever heard of getting up at 4:00 a.m. to put a twenty-four-pound steak in the oven—let alone trying to stuff one? No more fighting over the drumsticks, agonizing between white or dark meat—no frugal Scandinavian guilt over throwing away the turkey carcass when you know thriftier cooks boil theirs for homemade soup. No worries about finding a roasting pan large enough to fit a small Volkswagen, reaching optimum internal meat temperature, or basting. Do you own a baster? The last time I saw mine, I think it was in Wee Jack's toy box.

Serving steak also puts an end to another dilemma: Which is better, fresh turkey or frozen? A frozen turkey is cheaper but infinitely more intimidating. You not only have to cook it "so the juices run clear," you must first thaw it properly so your family and guests needn't make a post-Thanksgiving trip to the emergency room, which would destroy forever your reputation as a good cook. Fresh turkeys are also more expensive. The closer it gets to Thanksgiving, the more scarce they become—probably due to the culinarily challenged who waited too long and ran out of time to properly thaw a frozen turkey.

With steak, you merely thaw it in the refrigerator overnight (unless you're grilling one "fresh"), or if necessary, pop it into the microwave on defrost for a few minutes. *Voila!*—throw that hunk of beef on the barby.

The best part of serving steak for Thanksgiving? No leftovers. Have you ever heard of whipping up a batch of steak hotdish? Steak tetrazini? Or creamed steak on toast? It's unheard of. At my house, the words "Who wants the last piece of steak?" always precedes a fork-fight—may the hungriest man/woman/teen/toddler win.

The state legislature once addressed the leftover problem, but I don't think they fully realized what they were up against. It was labeled the "Potluck Bill"—and it guaranteed that the State Health Department couldn't stick its nose under the lids of the dish-towel-covered offerings at Minnesota's potlucks. They didn't realize that the potluck is the best place for wanton dispersal of leftovers.

When Big Jack, Wee Jack, and the saplings have become too familiar with the contents of the refrigerator—a twelve-course turkey dinner tucked lovingly into Rubberware containers and shoved to the back of the shelves—I can take the tidbits (well-disguised) to a potluck. Strangers will rave over the same dinner if it is strategically camouflaged into something creamy, well-seasoned, and best of all—from someone else's kitchen. Remember when you were a child and the toys at someone else's house were always more fun? The same principle holds true with leftovers.

The Pilgrim wives who contributed to the first Thanksgiving (sans the benefit of a Turkey Hotline) deserve their own national monument. They had journeyed under extreme hardship to an unknown destination and attempted to carve out homes in an untamed land filled with hidden dangers. When Goody Goodwife prepared a few too many fowl on Thanksgiving, I wonder if she had difficulty passing off turkey leftovers for the third straight day? And without so much as a can of cream-of-something soup to toss into the mix. The truth is the only reason the Pilgrims didn't have steak for the first Thanksgiving was because they didn't have room for cows on the Mayflower.

And now we're paying for it.

∽ • ∾

❧ The Wheels on the Bus ❧

In a lifetime, the average American spends six months sitting at traffic lights, eight months opening junk mail, two years trying to reach someone by phone, five years waiting in line (that figure must be longer if you frequent the post office!), and twenty-five years sleeping.

I've spent 174 full days of my life riding a school bus.

Why so long? Chalk it up to losing the school bus lottery. Due to our geographical location—otherwise known as "living out in the boonies"—we were always the first ones on the bus and the last ones to get off. A two-hour round trip, not counting time spent sitting in parking lots changing buses, adds up.

We lived so far from town, they used to call our dad, a school board member, to check on weather conditions out in our neck of the woods. We kids knew the call was coming. We would pantomime frantically in the background while Dad was on the phone. He never caved in or altered his assessment according to our gesticulations, but calmly and truthfully answered, "It's coming down pretty good out here," or "No, it's starting to taper off."

Once, when school hadn't been canceled, Dad still was concerned that our bus might get stuck, so he decided to drive us to school. The buses all made it to school. We couldn't get out of our driveway.

Over the years, we broke in a motley crew of bus drivers—a process akin to breaking in a new substitute teacher. They ranged from young men trying to make an extra buck, to the older owner of the bus line. "Sam" (all names have been changed, so no one can try to seek retribution) was one of my favorites. He always had a smile or a joke, and he called me "Peanut." Another one, Howard, is now the husband of one of my friends—he had to have been one of our younger drivers. Ralph used to take his corners so fast, he left bus driving behind and went on to an illustrious career driving an ambulance—true story.

I used to drive my kids to school, and I honestly don't know how bus drivers do it—especially with treacherous Minnesota winter driving conditions. They're essentially babysitting sixty kids while simultaneously operating thirteen-tons of heavy equipment. Try it some time.

When I rode the schoolbus, it was populated with colorful students, like Peter the bottomless pit, Sally the quick-change artist, and Rosalie the counterfeit queen.

Mom had made me a new purse with a long, serpentine chain handle. I loved that trendy chain. But when I put it on the bus seat beside me, the chain fell through the crack of the seat and Peter, the starving, snot-nosed kid in the seat behind me, chewed through the chain. All I can imagine is he must have gotten up too late for breakfast that day.

Sally used the relative privacy of the backseat to slip a shorter skirt on under the one she was wearing. Then she hid the longer, unfashionable garment under the seat to be retrieved in the afternoon. Her scheme backfired once. Our bus was taken in for repairs. I'm sure she had some explaining to do when she arrived home wearing different clothes than that morning.

Rosalie practiced forging parents' signatures on tardy notes and absence passes—she was pretty good. With one glance, she could effectively reproduce the sweeps and flourishes of the most challenging John Hancock.

Our bus rides were safe for the most part and with a big brother and sister on board, I never needed to worry about bullying. Most pranks were of the harmless variety—except for one. "Who lit the firecracker!!" will go down in infamy. I've never seen our bus driver so angry.

Were those seemingly unending school bus days wasted time? Yes, the days were long, and in the dead of winter, we often rode the bus in semidarkness. Yes, it was crowded, especially near the end of the route when we were packed in three to a seat and you could easily tell who had bacon for breakfast or who forgot to brush their teeth. But at the same time, it also gave us a little extra time to catch up on homework or cram for the test we faced once we arrived at school—and we benefited from having older students on board to help out when the assignment was too difficult. Best of all, the friendships forged within the close confines of school bus seats lasted throughout our school days—and beyond.

~ The Thrill of the Hunt ~

I tripped over a mountainous heap piled inside my back door and thought my husband was leaving me. In a way, he was—for a weekend of duck hunting. Since fall weather is predictable for its unpredictability, Jack prepares for everything from sunburn and mosquitoes to blizzards and hypothermia. While gingerly skirting the edges, trying not to trip and send the heap cascading down around me, I noted the following:

1. Warm weather camouflage pants, shirt, jacket, hat, and light hiking boots.

2. Same entire outfit as above only for cold weather, including heavy Sorel boots.

3. Two shotguns (in case one jams, falls in the swamp or gets left on the bumper at the Holiday gas station during a pit stop).

4. Five boxes of shells, each containing twenty-five rounds. Assuming each hunter in the party brings the same, I was led to speculate who would be louder—the hunters? Or Camp Ripley?

5. Camouflage binoculars.

6. Camera to record the hunt for posterity. Don't forget to label those duck photos immediately, or the only way you'll be able to tell later what year it was will be by the gradually receding hairlines and expanding waistlines of the hunters. If

they were photographed with full-camo caps and coats, it will be darn near impossible.

7. One large camo duffle stuffed with who-knows-what, but it squawked at me when I nudged it. I learned it was one of two duck calls. Are those brought in duplicate for the same reasons as the shotguns, perhaps?

There was a similar-sized pile in the garage:

1. Three dozen decoys. Multiply this by four additional hunters and there won't be enough unoccupied water left in the bay for the real ducks.

2. Extra-large camo life jacket. I was glad to see this, especially after viewing the chilling public service announcement of the hunting dog viewed from underwater, paddling around the overturned boat.

3. Duck boat, oars, seats, anchor, cooler, roof rack, etc.

4. Handwarmers, footwarmers, bunwarmers. Really!?

5. Thermal rubber gloves for plucking wet, icy decoys out of frigid swamp water.

Surely safaris to darkest Africa couldn't have more paraphernalia than this, but the trophies they return with were in monstrous proportions compared to the handful of ducks I was expecting.

Some hunters also use a trained dog to hunt. Of course, you could follow our example. Find a really good Lab breeder, get a pup who turns out to be too frisky to hunt, then be too busy to work with her so she ends up as a family dog—which every truly dedicated hunter knows spoils a good gun dog forever. But in our case it's too late. She's now a non-hunter because the kids and I have grown so attached to her we flat-out told Jack, "If she gets lost in the wetland and you come home without her, well, just don't come home."

After one such hunting weekend where the amount of accumulated gear hardly justified bringing home two scrawny, plucked ducks, I decided to calculate how much was spent trying to bag such slim pickin's. I soon discovered that the worst blow you can deal to a hunter's ego, is to present him with the cost per pound of his quarry.

I figured in the full retail prices (Jack isn't known for his bargain hunting) of the afore-mentioned gear, plus dog, and gas to get to the northern duck lakes. Although we're surrounded on all sides by water, Minnesotans always have to go farther north, don't ask me why.

Just to be a good sport, I left out the cost of depreciation and wear and tear on the vehicle getting into and out of the secluded spots often located on isolated logging roads not known for their maintenance records. I could have been really mean-spirited and included the cost of having a four-wheel-drive vehicle to get into those spots, but not wanting to depress him beyond recovery, I kindly left that five-figure amount out of the total.

Groceries to cover his share of one of the weekend's meals—haute cuisine like Beanies n' Weanies, Spam, pork hocks, beef jerky, and a case of Pepcid—brought the ten-year average to $738 per year or $46.17 per pound of duck.

I handed Jack my figures as I left for the fish market. I told him I was going hunting. The way I see it, at those prices, I could bag a couple of pretty dandy-looking lobsters—and still come out ahead.

~ • ~

~ Life Is a Bear Hunt ~

I was worried. Jack was going bear hunting, and I had a dreadful thought: What will I do if he gets one? Don't get me wrong—I am not a novice hunting wife. From day one, I knew I was married to a hunter. One of our first social events as an engaged couple was the annual Game Dinner—that bastion of culinary delights gorged in the company of Jack's hunting buddies. I'd sampled squirrel, eaten elk, downed duck a l'orange, gulped grouse, and even tasted other tidbits about which I wisely chose to remain ignorant of their animal-of-origin.

In the early years, I'd accompanied Jack pheasant hunting. He didn't have a hunting dog, so I volunteered to go ahead and flush out the game. It sounded like a nice walk on a fall afternoon—a chance for companionship and a little togetherness. He forgot to tell me the part about hitting the deck (or in this case, sharp, stubbly straw) when I flushed a bird. Whenever we travel south and pass the pheasant field—now paved over and developed into a county government complex—it brings back fond memories of togetherness mingled with several . . . shall I say . . . hasty words.

Another time we planned to go trap shooting—it sounded like fun. The clay pigeons were flung automatically. I didn't need to flush anything and it was another sunny, fall day in God's Country. Before we left, Jack opened the box to show me the clay pigeons. They weren't at all what I'd pictured—wouldn't you think they'd be pigeon-shaped? Jack laughed so hard, I lost a little more of my quickly waning interest in becoming his hunting companion.

But as a newlywed wife, determined to build togetherness by sharing every experience, I volunteered to help Jack pluck a few freshly shot ducks. Among the menagerie of limp fowl was a snow goose. Thinking that the larger feathers of a goose would be easier to pluck than a duck's smaller ones, I chose the goose. As we worked in the dank basement of our tiny house, with its damp concrete walls and single light bulbs dangling from the low-raftered ceiling, I became aware of an aroma—more accurately, a stench.

"Uh, honey," I asked hesitantly, "is it supposed to smell like this?"

"It's all right," Jack encouraged from across the room. "It just takes getting used to."

I pluckily plucked on.

"Jack, it smells really bad. Will you come here for a minute?" Just then I pulled out a handful of feathers, along with a large hunk of green, gangrenous gooseflesh. Jack appeared at my side in time for me to thrust the rotting, previously shot bird into his hands. I fled upstairs, clutching my stomach.

To this day, I won't pluck a duck, filet a fish, or dissect a deer. I'll cook the finished, well-washed flesh, but that's where I draw the line.

Back to the bear.

Last year, we had a huge freezer. It was large enough to hold Jack's deer/ducks/grouse, our son's deer, my father-in-law's deer, deer hides salted and frozen until we had them tanned—plus garden vegetables, strawberry freezer jam, and assorted groceries. But this summer our dinosaur-relic, energy-gulping freezer went gasping into extinction, as all good dinosaurs eventually do. Before the venison burger thawed, we rushed out and purchased the cheapest, most-efficient freezer available—which also has one-eighth the capacity of its predecessor.

That's when I worried: Where will I fit a bear? (Okay, half a bear after splitting it with his hunting buddy.) I'd already frozen dozens of pints of green beans, the broccoli was ready to harvest, and we needed room for this fall's inevitable deer/ducks/grouse/hides.

Calmly explaining all this to Jack, I concluded, ". . . so where am I going to put a bear?"

"Let's just take this one bear at a time," was his best offer.

I sputtered in frustration at his retreating back. To me, security means knowing exactly how each piece in my life-puzzle fits—no surprises. Like Crispian's Crispian in Wee Jack's book, *Mister Dog*, I like "everything in its own place—the cup in the saucer, the chair under the table, the stars in the heavens, the moon in the sky . . ."

I wanted to add, "and the bear in a large, roomy freezer."

Maybe you guessed it—Jack and his buddy were skunked—in a manner of speaking. They didn't get "their" bear. Our small, efficient freezer cheerfully accepted whatever I crammed into it throughout the harvesting and hunting seasons and beyond. And I'm learning to take each day, each hunt, each challenge as it comes. Take life—one bear at a time.

ᔕ • ᔐ

~ North Woods Barbie ~
The New and Improved Pink Aisle

Although winter is closer than we think, and visions of sugarplums might be dancing in some children's heads, our house is always a sugarplum-free zone. Sugarplums sound too feminine for the likes of my all-male household. Wee Jack even calls the Barbie department at the toy store "the pink aisle" and he won't let so much as the shadows of our shopping cart's wheels turn in its direction.

When I was a girl, the only Barbie dolls I played with belonged to my friends. The anatomically correct Barbie wasn't allowed in our house. Now that I'm an adult, I've found that mothers of other girls felt the same way. Ironically, the dolls I was allowed to play with were trolls. Now that I've begun to battle middle-age spread, I doubt that the dumpy, bumpy troll figure was a very good role model either.

The fascination with the Barbie doll seems timeless, but I can't help thinking that Mattel is missing out on a very lucrative demographic by not factoring the up-north consumer into its marketing strategy. It's quite simple, really. Barbie needs to be expanded with a North Woods Barbie collection. (You heard it here, first. All rights reserved!)

• North Woods Barbie sports a pink-and-black plaid flannel shirt, pink wool slacks, tiny pink Sorels, a bomber hat with pink rabbit-fur earflaps, and a trendy down jacket. Instead of a jacuzzi, North Woods Barbie is equipped with a little sauna and a fake snowbank to roll in once she works up a sweat. Which raises an interesting point—is Barbie even capable of working up a sweat? Available in her accessories line is a four-wheeler—batteries not included—for hauling home the deer, delivering a cord of firewood, or bringing home the bacon to fry up in the pan.

• The concept for Boundary Waters Canoe Area (BWCA) Barbie was born when a friend told me he took his daughter on the canoe trails for the first time when she was only seven years old. Her Barbie collection came along on the trip and their fair tresses got wet when she made them dive from the gunwales of the canoe. The BWCA Barbie comes with a pink Duluth pack on a titanium frame, a tiny water-filtration kit, a pink birchbark canoe, and a Colewoman lantern. Clothing accessories include a full-body pink mesh bug suit for the pesky blackfly season.

• A little closer to home is Beanhole Days Barbie—created to celebrate the annual festival in Pequot Lakes, Minnesota. Of course, Barbie has been crowned Queen Bean. In addition to her crown, her highness's ensemble includes the official Beanhole t-shirt and a tiny pink fannypack that holds a wee bottle of Beano. She totes a pink-striped mesh folding chair to be used while she waits in line for the delectable beans to be raised from the hole where the cast-iron kettle cooked the beans overnight.

• Turtle Race Barbie is ready for anything. In case the turtle brokers come up empty-handed and can't field enough race-ready turtles, Turtle Race Barbie sports pink waders for rounding up her own tiny turtles, a can of non-toxic pink spray paint for marking which ones are hers, and several empty, tiny, pink strawberry ice cream buckets for toting home her stable of winners.

• Gull Lake's Ice Fishing Extravaganza Barbie wears her hot-pink-and-black camouflage snowmobile suit leftover from deer-hunting season. It can be mixed and matched with the ensemble from North Woods Barbie (Sorels, bomber hat, etc.), and also includes pink leather chopper mittens and tiny packets of genuine imitation hand- and footwarmers. (The real thing would melt her molded fingers and toes.) She'll never win the fishing contest, however. It drives Ken nuts, but politically correct Barbie will only catch and release.

• When Fishing Extravaganza Barbie isn't at the ice fishing contest, she might take a daytrip north to check out the goings-on at the Eelpout Festival in Walker, Minnesota. She might try flinging a tiny pink 'pout, chugging a thimble or two of root beer, and building her own 'Pout Shack from sheets of pre-cut pink styrofoam (some assembly required).

• Not to neglect the warmer seasonal activities, deluxe Paul Bunyan Trail Barbie comes complete with rollerblades, a pink mountain bike that really works (some assembly required), a pink Nalgene water bottle to clip onto her belt, along with a money pouch to hold her play money for shopping at all the great stores along the trail.

• For the bargain-hunting Barbie fans, we offer Garage Sale/Flea Market Barbie with interchangeable accessories that can be used for either venue. Pink card table and matching striped awning, signs with letters that can be altered to fit the sale occasion, a pre-programmed sound chip with phrases like, "No early sales," "Yes, I can go lower on that," or "No, that's my best price." Flea Market Barbie also comes with a miniature bag of sugar-coated mini-donuts because she's more concerned with having a good time than watching her figure.

I think area mothers will appreciate the functional, more creative play qualities of the North Woods Barbie. What do you think, Mom?

☙ • ❧

It's All in the Details

All children are artists. The problem is how to remain an artist once he grows up. —Pablo Picasso

I've heard that life is what happens when we're making other plans. If that's true, how do we capture the moments and remember them? Sometimes it means taking the road less traveled or paying attention to the tiny details along the way.

When my young sapling chose to sit on the opposite side of the back seat on a drive into town, he said, "It looked like a different world." It was our road—he'd just never noticed it from that perspective before. A friend once polished the light globes in her living room after a cleaning hiatus and could hardly believe how they sparkled. She told me she had forgotten that they weren't frosted glass! Pay attention to the details. Have you ever tried to find a substitute for a twist tie when you really needed one? Small things can be important.

While I am the official writer in the family, the literary gifts of the entire family were recently on display in the "Refrigerator Collection." I had purchased a North Woods Words refrigerator magnet set, thinking I would get a little use out of it and have some fun. After a recent holiday, I was surprised to see the random poetry my Jackpine Savages had assembled throughout the weekend. I am still reluctant to take it down, because the discovery gave me such joy.

It's all in the details that pop up like signposts along the road of life. Remember that even small things—clean glass, car windows, twist ties, and fridge magnets—can make a difference.

Write it or forget it.

~ Boochie! ~

Our family tradition of "Boochie" was imported from an episode of the *Perfect Strangers* sitcom from the late-1980s. Balki, a sheepherder, moved from the Mediterranean island of Mypos to live with his cousin, Larry, in Chicago. (Balki doesn't call himself a "shepherd." He is a "sheepherder," which is uttered in Balki's inimitable Myposian accent.)

One of the Mypos games Balki taught Larry was "Boochie," which is a form of tag. Instead of saying "Tag, you're it," a player says, "Boochie!" and the chase begins. Players never know when a game begins or ends and players can be ambushed at any time.

When we adopted Boochie at our house, even the dog got into the act and could "boochie" a player with her tail. Our family has refined Boochie over the years with countless variations and rules. Rules such as, Dad can't Boochie our son when the child is being tucked into bed—there has to be a "safe zone" somewhere! Just to keep the peace, I seldom play. Someone is also needed to referee.

I bought the *Perfect Strangers* DVD for Christmas and was surprised how short the actual Boochie episode was, yet it provided our family with many fun and happy memories. It's amazing how something so insignificant can do so much toward family bonding.

Boochie is still alive and well at our house. Celebrate your family traditions—no matter how oddball they may seem to others. Families grow up, but memories will always remain. What are some of yours?

And just so you know . . . because you read this story . . . Boochie!

Ages & Stages

Growing up as a country mouse meant playing with my little sister because my other playmates lived too far away. Our mother had specific ideas about appropriate play toys for little girls. We weren't allowed to have Barbie dolls, so we dressed and made up storylines for our collection of trolls. Mom was ahead of her time in thinking that Barbie projected a poor body image for girls to try and mimic. However, I've always questioned what made the troll body image more appropriate?

When I was in college the first time, it was quite a few years ago. How long ago, you ask? Let's just say I used to play the role of the ingenue in theater productions. Back then, when I took stage make-up class, I had a hard time creating old-age makeup on my face. About twenty years later, when I was making up my face for a story-telling event, I had no problem making myself up to look old. What changed? I now had wrinkles to follow. Just draw along the lines—piece of cake.

And then I returned to college as an adult to finish my degree and get my master's. It was funny, when I filled out the last FAFSA for our older sons I rejoiced that I wouldn't have to do it again until our youngest was ready. Two years later, I was filling out the FAFSA for myself.

One of our sons jokingly said, "Mom cut her hair short, wants to take up kayaking, went back to college, and bought a new car. If the car is red, it's definitely a mid-life crisis."

I like to think of it as a mid-life inventory. I won't go looking for a trophy husband, and buying a convertible isn't really my style. But what is wrong with making changes in our lives? At any age?

By the way, the car wasn't red, it was gray, but it got thirty-two miles per gallon, so who cares?

☙ • ❧

Winter

~ Survival of the Fittest ~

Reality television changed forever when *Survivor* first aired in primetime. I've always considered it a cross between *Do You Want to be a Millionaire?* and *Gilligan's Island*.

In the initial episodes, sixteen people lived on a deserted, tropical island off the Borneo coast. Deserted, that is, except for the camera crew filming them twenty-four hours a day.

They were required to construct their own shelters and find food and water, while fending off the occasional wild pig. And one more thing, all applicants—through rigorous physical- and mental-health screening—must be in "good mental health."

I have three things to say about *Survivor*.

First, I think most Midwesterners could qualify. After all, didn't we all survive the 2013 *Winter That Wouldn't Quit*? What's so difficult about a few weeks on a tropical-island paradise? We made it through the cabin-fever blues that stretched nearly into June, which qualifies all of us in the good mental-health category. Of course, I might have to deduct a few points under "excellent physical health," because I survived said-blues by munching too many leftover Christmas cookies, while snowed in for the fourth time. In reality, can anyone who is seriously thinking about tackling this venture be considered in full control of his mental faculties?

The producers also look for "strong-willed, outgoing, adventurous individuals who are adaptable to new environments, with interesting lifestyles, backgrounds, and personalities."

Let's break my qualifications down by category:

• Strong-willed—I'm a stubborn Swede married to an equally stubborn German and it's worked since 1977. Need I say more?

• Outgoing—People who know me now can't believe I was a former shy person. While many people equate public speaking on par with death, I'll jump up to speak at the drop of a stocking hat. However, as a child, I almost choked to death on a black jellybean because I was too Minnesota Nice to tell my friend's father that I loathe black jellybeans, so I tried to swallow one whole.

• Adventurous—Living in the Midwest, we make our own excitement when the wind chill hits eighty degrees below zero. True adventure is going to the market for a gallon of milk when the frozen car engine squeals louder than the Lab when her tail gets stepped on.

• Adaptable to new environments—This is the one category I win hands down. If I can navigate the terrain between a grandchild's upended trunk of Legos and unearthing the rancid locker-room athletic socks of Teen Jack—set me on a pristine, sugar sand beach and I'll emerge victorious.

Plus, the island is supposed to be uninhabited, yet the contestants will be filmed twenty-four hours a day? Picture the scenario. After a long day of monitoring an increasingly unruly mob of Survivors—who soon come to resemble, not the cast of a primetime television show, but rather the sniveling brats in *Lord of the Flies*—the camera crew settles down for a wienie roast topped off with s'mores. Meanwhile, the commando unit of starving Survivors descends on the crew's camp, ties them up with camera cables, and carries off all their Spam.

Now that it's been determined that any Minnesotan worth his/her roadsalt would satisfy the requirements, let's look at my second point—Location, Location, Location.

The applicants for the premier episodes of *Survivor* applied at the amusement park at the Mall of America. Could they have picked a wimpier registration site? I think prospective survivors should be pre-screened at Camp Ripley, where the *Survivor* wannabes can run an obstacle course tougher than scavenging their way through the food court and navigating Legoland.

And if the producers want to film survival, why don't they set the contestants down in the middle of a boreal forest with only a book of matches? They could construct their own igloos in sub-zero January temperatures or build mosquito-proof lean-tos in the dog days of August. Pick a month, any month, and our Midwestern terrain would be infinitely more challenging than a tropical-island paradise.

The truth is the CBS *Survivor* television show will never tape its series out in my neck of the woods. Used to a steady diet of skimpy bikini-clad women and shirtless men in a tropical setting, the audience would never tune in to watch castaways bundled up in parkas, pack boots, mufflers, gloves, and stocking hats.

What would they do for challenges—have the contestants stand on iceblocks and the last one to plunge into the drink wins? Or mush a sled dog team around a forested path—the first one to the finish line takes home a snowmobile? Perhaps the survivors could drop a fish line through a hole in a fish house and try to catch enough crappies (small panfish) to feed the shivering tribe. The first challenge would definitely have to be for the prize of fire—the losers would be permitted to perform camp chores for the winners to catch a few errant waves of warmth, lest anyone suffers frostbite on national television and gives a black eye to the good name of reality TV.

And if you really want to talk survival—place them all in a couple of snow huts. But then again, maybe the ratings would go up. Much more survivor "cuddling" would take place and the audience would jam the *Survivor* chatroom with speculation on what is really going on in those zipped-together, down sleeping bags.

The tribe has spoken: *Brrrrr.*

Finally, the "applicants cannot be candidates for public office." I think they are eliminating the most-qualified candidate pool of prospective Survivors. Who better understands the physics of survival than politicians? In the early years, they should have put former governor Jesse Ventura on a desert island. He would have fit in, Rambo-style, like a character from his movie career. (And if survival requires scavenging for a wild-pig entree, who knows, he might even "find time to bleed.")

All in all, I think they are doing their contestant pool a great disservice by disqualifying politicians. These days, that just might be a good way to winnow out the few, the proud—the *Survivors*.

❧ The Gift Couch ❧
Or
Lessons Learned in the Hand-Me-Down School of Life

Trying to wed my husband's and my decorating tastes was like attempting a match between Martha Stewart and Jack London. Never the twain shall meet. Fortunately we have both a family room and a living room, so I don't have to draw a line down one room's center for His Side and Her Side.

His north woods family room runs to anything finned, furred, or feathered: duck and loon prints, old decoys, an old Schell beer can, antique shotgun shells, brass ducks, and the requisite mounted deer antlers. No ten-pointers—just a respectable collection that even includes a wimpy spike-buck.

My civilized living room contains the piano—okay, no one plays it, but it makes a nice, though unwieldy, shelf. An antique quilt draped across a chair, washboard propped up on the fireplace, Red Wing crock, old book collection—you get the picture.

He watches television reclined on the couch in his lair. I sit in my mother's antique rocking chair, reading and sipping raspberry tea. He never could comprehend my instant aversion to what I now grudgingly call our "gift couch."

From the moment I laid eyes on the earth-toned, brown tweedy sofa, it was dislike-at-first-sight. Forget for a moment that it perfectly complemented my beige living room carpeting. It deliberately flaunted the mud-colored effect I was desperately trying to avoid. We had built and carpeted our home in 1980—the year earth-tones were popular. I had foolishly bought into that fad and have been trying to minimize the damage ever since.

Even though the second-hand couch was free—lovingly donated by a relative who was getting new furniture—it would never be my favorite color. After a long two months, I learned to accept it. Rather graciously, too, I'd thought.

"We need extra seating, it is nice and big—I can slipcover it!" I rationalized.

I never dreamed the muddy monster was capable of reproduction. It singlehandedly spawned a perfect clone: a matching earth-toned loveseat. The truly well-meaning relative thought we would appreciate a matched set.

When the second piece was delivered and installed in my living room, it and its evil twin dwarfed the Americana collectibles I'd lovingly and painstakingly scrounged from flea markets and garage sales. My eyes unexpectedly filled with tears, to the surprise of my husband.

"I hated the first one. Now I've got two!" I blurted, surprised by the lingering couch-angst simmering just below the surface. I fled the room, vowing to shuffle them to the nether regions of the downstairs family room.

Suddenly the phrase, "Don't look a gift couch in the mouth," popped into my mind. In earlier days, the protocol for being given a horse meant you didn't pry open its jaws to inspect the teeth, to determine the age and value of the horse. It would be rude and inconsiderate. Did this mean I had to accept these couches at face value? Ignore their dubious colors? Shop for another slipcover?

I learned to appreciate them, after they were shipped downstairs to "his room." My living room now contains a new hand-me-down sectional in a light cream color. It brightens the room. It can seat half a gazillion people, and—I like it. Really . . .

Deck the Halls
Or
Anything Else Standing Still

Minnesota is a land of extremes. From cut-it-with-a-knife-sticky-humid-sweatbox summers—to freeze-your-tongue-on-a-pump-handle-double-digit-below-zero-windchill-winters. We have extremes of temperaments: polka-dancing, spicy-sausage-munching Germans to bottle-it-up-inside, "Pass the lutefisk, Lena," Swedes. (I'm only picking on those because I can lay claim to both in my lineage. Don't take it personally.) Then there are the extremes of Christmas decorating.

Remember the tree in Charlie Brown's Christmas? The spindly job with three bulbs and a leaning star on top? Except for the spindly part, if Jack had his way that's what our tree would resemble. As newlyweds, we instantly recognized our dissimilar tastes in Christmas decorating—due to the simple fact that I brought to the marriage eight handmade felt/sequined birds and six heirloom glass ornaments for the Christmas tree, and Jack contributed—zilch. We all know that the one with the most ornaments wins. Being on a limited newlywed budget, I can tell you exactly what we hung on our first tree, not counting said birds and glass balls.

- One strand of non-blinking, multi-colored lights.
- One strand of garland, white and gold.

- Six blue-and-white balls printed with sleigh ride scenes, purchased at Ben Franklin.
- Six "string tomatoes" (what I affectionately call those Styrofoam balls covered with shiny scarlet thread).

Not a single partridge in a pear tree! We have a photograph of a much-younger me posed in front of our tree. There was definitely more green than glitz!

I have taken over the task of decorating the Christmas tree for the simple reason that Jack wants to stop before it's finished. He will wrestle it freshly cut out of the woods (which is a story for another day), wrangle into the recalcitrant tree stand, drag it into the house, place it strategically in the appropriate room depending on whether we have sticky-fingered toddlers at the time (downstairs if we do, upstairs if we don't), place the angel on top, string the lights, replace missing bulbs, and restring the lights. Then I begin.

I now have a hope chest stuffed with Christmas ornaments and memorabilia, not counting my Christmas book collection stashed elsewhere. When the chest overflowed, I moved the excess into another box. When that burst at the seams, the decorations acquired a shelf on Jack's side of the closet. Perhaps a lean-to on the back of the house is next. When I have a garage sale, you'll never find a table of Christmas items for sale; they're sacred.

Remember those afore-mentioned sticky-fingered toddlers? Forget the fact that they're now taller than Jack. I still hang their glitter-paste-popsicle stick concoctions on our Christmas tree along with the purple crayon-coated stars with tinsel streamers and paper plate angels with rickrack-trimmed skirts they brought home from Sunday School. In addition to their Baby's First Christmas ornaments, I've also purchased an ornament each year for our Jack Pine saplings. We hang vacation souvenir ornaments (I have a fondness for pelicans) and ornaments given to us by family and friends. The kids and I discuss the heritage of each as it is hung on a fresh, pine-scented bough. They also have their elementary school photo ornaments or Wee Jack's from preschool. His teacher always photographed the kids after their naps, so most of W.J.'s look like they should have a number across his chest.

When the tree begins to list dangerously to the side where I placed the cookie-dough wreaths, Jack cautions, "Don't you think that's about enough?" He knows that trying to interfere is like coming between the shoppers and the bargains at a post-Christmas sale. I heedlessly produce two more boxes from the depths of the closet while humming, "I'm Dreaming of a White Christmas."

Jack knows I won't rest until the last clothespin reindeer with googly eyes is placed next to one of the remaining heirloom glass balls. And if the tree branches run out before the ornaments do—I've also been tried and found guilty of double-hanging.

I dig out the old Christmas albums to play on the turntable (youngsters ask your parents for the definitions of "album" and "turntable") while we decorate the tree. And we munch on cookies made with real butter and cream cheese using my mom's old spritz cookie maker. I disposed of the rosette maker after my family dubbed those efforts, "grease cookies."

I firmly believe that Christmas is the perfect time to unearth the memories and polish them in our hearts till they sparkle anew. As they hang a yarn-strung paper ball, embellished with a pasted-on school photo of a gap-toothed kindergartner, my strapping saplings remind me, "We're not just hanging ornaments—we're hanging memories."

Merry Christmas!

Dinosaurs and Other Extinct Species

While attempting to unclutter my miniscule home office, I became distracted by an article in the "To File" pile (so much for New Year's resolutions). It was a clipping from a 1950s high-school home-economics textbook that prepared girls to be good wives (*see below*).

I could take days exploring each of these "dinosaurs" in depth. Let me elaborate on a few, then you can giggle hysterically over the rest at your leisure.

Dinner: Since the 1950s, our lives have spun so far out of control in the areas of jobs, sports, school activities, and so-called leisure, we're lucky if we eat at home at all, let alone together. I pity the poor mothers of the '50s. They didn't enjoy the option of choosing between "running for the border" and "having it your way." Frozen dinners were limited to soggy pot pies or cardboard and gravy TV dinners.

Our house is a pit stop for a quick Digiorno's between school, ballfield, office, and the mall. Here in the north woods, we pride ourselves on having escaped the rat race. The truth is, we're as busy as suburban folks. We still have to drive forty-five minutes one way for the 10:00 p.m. hockey practice—our drive time just has better scenery. We also have the additional hazard of kamikaze deer, raccoons, skunks—perhaps even cougars, depending on where you live.

Clutter: Nothing wears me out faster than browsing through an "organize your home, life, future, total existence" type of book. The charts, schedules, lists, and recipes for "Making Your Own Windshield Washer Fluid," leave me with two responses. Either my eyes glaze into a catatonic state at the sheer mass of energy such an undertaking would involve, or I wonder, *Don't these people have a life?*

Personally, I've adopted as my motto the cross-stitch ditty that begins: "Cleaning and scrubbing can wait 'til tomorrow . . . For babies grow up, I've learned to my sorrow." The truth is, they *are* too big for the rocking chair—they're now old enough to help clean up the clutter they've helped create for so many years. Of course, that's providing I can catch them between school, sports practice (we must encourage physical fitness), homework (keep up the GPA to get into a respectable college), and sleeping. (They still look so cute when they're asleep, I don't have the heart to wake them to clean their rooms.)

That leaves five minutes every third Tuesday of the fourth month of odd-numbered years, not counting leap year, for them to catch up on cleaning their rooms, taking out the garbage, and shoveling snow. Did I say odd years? It's now 2014? Oh, well . . .

Those rules applied to our two strapping saplings. When Wee Jack (now Teen Jack) was a tot, his favorite contribution to the combined clutter was upending the laundry basket, which held his ball collection, to get at the basketball on the bottom. We all had to work hard to teach him to pick up his toys, but it didn't help that he looked so gosh-darn cute sitting in his toy box after he emptied the contents onto my semi-clean floor.

Prepare Yourself/Make Him Comfortable: These quaint bits of advice fall with a thud into the "you've got to be kidding" category. At the end of Jack's day, I've usually just gotten home myself and crawled into comfy sweats before nuking something frozen for dinner. I won't even touch the "man on a pedestal" image this propagates. Suffice it to say that if I began treating Jack this way, he'd either call the guys in white coats or begin searching for a bottle stashed in the couch cushions. And if I offered to take his shoes (providing I summoned enough courage to want to touch them), Jack would turn white and back out the door while mumbling incoherently, "What did you do to the car now?"

Dinosaurs became extinct because they were too big to fit into the microwave. For similarly practical reasons, these "dinosaurs" were also doomed to extinction.

"Timeless Tips for 1950s Homemakers" (excerpted from Encyclopedia for Homemakers)

1. ***Have dinner ready.*** *Plan ahead, even the night before, to have a delicious meal on time. This is a way of letting him know that you have been thinking about him and are concerned about his needs. Most men are hungry when they come home and the prospects of a good meal are part of the warm welcome needed.*

2. ***Prepare yourself.*** *Take fifteen minutes to rest so you will be refreshed when he arrives. Touch-up your makeup, put a ribbon in your hair, and be fresh-looking. He has just been with a lot of work-weary people. Be a little gay and a little more interesting. His boring day may need a lift.*

3. ***Clear away the clutter.*** *Make one last trip through the main part of the house just before your husband arrives, gathering up schoolbooks, toys, papers, etc. Then run a dustcloth over the tables. Your husband will feel he has reached a haven of rest and order, it will give you a lift, too.*

4. ***Prepare the children.*** *Take a few minutes to wash the children's hands and faces (if they are small), comb their hair, and if necessary, change their clothes. They are little treasures and he would like to see them playing the part.*

5. ***Minimize all noise.*** *At the time of his arrival, eliminate all noise of the washer, dryer, dishwasher, or vacuum. Try to encourage the children to be quiet. Be happy to see him. Greet him with a warm smile and be glad to see him.*

6. ***Some don'ts.*** *Don't greet him with problems or complaints. Don't complain if he's late for dinner. Count this as minor compared with what he might have gone through that day at work.*

7. ***Make him comfortable.*** *Have him lean back in a comfortable chair or suggest he lie down in the bedroom. Have a cool or warm drink ready for him. Arrange his pillow and offer to take off his shoes. Speak in a low, soft, soothing and pleasant voice. Allow him to relax/unwind.*

8. ***Listen to him.*** *Never complain if he does not take you out to dinner or other places of entertainment. Instead, try to understand his world of strain and pressure, and his need to be home and relax.*

9. ***The goal.*** *Try to make your home a place of peace and order, where your husband can renew himself in body and spirit.*

Some Have It. Some Don't.

We're fast approaching the dead of winter. The holidays are tinsel-strewn memories, and Valentine's Day exists only on the shelves of ambitious chainstores. Lest Lake Country folks go stark raving mad and run out into the snow wearing nothing but birthday suits (and sans the sauna first), many take up hobbies to see them through cabin-fever season. A few actively embrace winter's charms: skiing, snowshoeing, and snowmobiling. Others prefer more sedentary pursuits: quilting, fly-tying, and putting another log on the fire. Me? I lean more towards sedentary, while still avoiding anything involving needles, pointy hooks, and flames.

I'll never be a crafty person. I don't mean "devious"—the jury is still out on that interpretation—but rather the ability to construct a motorhome using little more than recycled Styrofoam, milk jugs, and a few toothpicks. My family is grateful knowing they'll never be dragged kicking and screaming to a fourteen-acre craft fair so that I can buy stuff and come up with a few new ideas to try at home.

I attribute this anti-craft mindset to early adolescence. When I was in junior high, the girls took home economics class and the boys took wood shop and metal shop and leather shop. I always wondered why anything with the word "shop" in the class title was designated for the male gender. It stands to reason it should fall more under female territory.

The year they decided to let the girls take the classes that were traditionally boys-only was a revolutionary break with tradition. I didn't do too badly. I still use the cookie sheet I made (I doubt if the boys made cookie sheets), the wooden fish was given to my parents, and the leather belt is moldering in one of my son's closets.

I probably fared better in shop class than in home economics. When we studied sewing, my favorite tool was the seam-ripper. It wasn't for lack of having a suitable role model. My mother was, is, and always will be the world's greatest seamstress. She once made a man's three-piece suit, for goodness sake. That's not a project you whip out the first time you exit a fabric store. Granted, back then it was cheaper to make clothing from patterns we'd selected from the Butterick or Simplicity books—at least that's what we were taught. As a teen-ager, I turned my back on home-constructed clothing forever the day my two-piece swimsuit fell apart in mixed company. And that's all I'm going to say on *that* subject.

Even though I've given up on being a seamstress, I think I accidentally discovered my creative calling. When I was a child I used to play with my mother's button collection. My favorite was a bunny button, and I've been searching for one ever since. Since I'm an inveterate collector, at a recent flea market I couldn't pass up a great buy on Miracle Whip jars filled with buttons.

Although my newly acquired stash proved to be bunny-button-less, I tried to think of something clever to do with a few hundred buttons. Frugal Scandinavian collectors always try to justify their hoardings. My favorite denim jacket, purchased for a song at another flea market because I seldom shop retail, struck me as rather plain. I began attaching colorful buttons in funky, random patterns across its back and pockets. My family thought the snow and cold had finally gotten to me, but for the first time in my adulthood, I felt latent stirrings of creativity deep within my frostbitten soul.

One day I forgot my coat at the library, and fearing it may have been stolen, was relieved to find it still there. My saplings asked which coat I'd forgotten. I replied, "My button denim jacket."

"That explains why no one took it," they said, rolling their eyes.

I don't think they suspect anything. At the bottom of my sock drawer, I've hidden rough sketches of buttons dancing like raindrops across the shower curtain and a button collage of loons on the Savage mailbox. The good news is, I still have a few hundred buttons left. When fears of Y2K came around back in January 2000 and I was worried the fabric stores wouldn't be able to get shipments of buttons, I stocked up. I've also stockpiled books. If the library computer is ever unable to access my account and I've nothing to read, I would have to resort to playing with needles, pointy hooks, and fire.

༄ • ༄

'Tis the Season...
To Go Overboard

A good friend called the other day and invited me to lunch at her home. Before I could stop myself, I uttered those four irrepressible little words, "What can I bring?"

What sacred Minnesota tradition makes us feel we can't show up at someone's house unless one arm is longer than the other? It must be traced to our pioneer ancestors. Provisions were scarce on the frontier, and it might have been considered rude and overbearing to expect a friend to feed you without contributing to the repast.

Okay, so Minnesota Nice dictates we are never rude or overbearing, and we're not lacking the bare necessities—but most of us wallow in our wants.

When my friend called, I was in the midst of baking twelve dozen Christmas cookies for a cookie exchange. None of us needed a larger assortment from which to nibble and add pounds, but it seemed like the thing to do—another item to cross off our master "We Did It All" holiday lists. We dutifully traded recipes like our kids swapped baseball cards. I didn't admit that the rest of the year my baking consists of a tube of cookie dough from the dairy case. "My name is Jacqueline and I've had an ongoing affair with the Pillsbury Doughboy."

Since we need something to wash down the cookies, the other irrepressible words are, "Would you like a cup of coffee?" Maybe you've already had five cups and the carafe is in the dishwasher—if someone drops in, you quickly brew up a fresh pot.

Coffee choices themselves are overwhelming. In addition to caff/decaf, any good Scandinavian should be able to make a stiff cup of egg coffee. I think one friend's recipe even calls for a warm egg, straight from the chicken, for best results. There are those who lace theirs with cream and sugar, Turkish coffee (they throw out the water and just boil down the grounds)—and I won't go into the espresso craze: tall/short/skinny/fat/latte/mocha/cappuccino/caff/decaf . . . ad nauseum.

Speaking of nauseum—one coffee fad comes from Indonesia. "The Coffee Critic" website reports that there is a small catlike marsupial, called the *paradoxurus*, that climbs coffee trees and eats the ripest coffee "cherries." The beans "come through the digestion process fairly intact," and the "Kopi Luwak" beans are harvested, washed (I hope!), and sold—at a whopping three or four *hundred* dollars a pound. Apparently "the enzymes in the animal's stomach add something unique to the coffee's flavor through fermentation."

I don't expect Kopi Luwak coffee to catch on in the north woods. According to Jack, "There's no way I'm gonna drink coffee that's come out some animal's poop chute."

Besides eating and drinking, another holiday overindulgence is shopping. I shop for Christmas throughout the year, then smugly announce to anyone who asks (and even many who don't), that my shopping is finished by the end of August.

At least that's my plan until the thermometer begins its steady decline. During the in-between season before the lakes freeze and there isn't enough snow to play in, I need something to do. So when the book-sized edition of the local paper with the day-after-Thanksgiving sales lands on my front doorstep, my well-laid gift-giving plans go right out the back door. I never realized that Great-aunt Ruth couldn't live without that gizmo until I saw it in the advertising supplement.

Advertising is also sometimes good for a laugh. Wee Jack isn't so wee anymore, but when he was smaller, I was amused by the ads for infant sportswear. What sports—besides long-distance spitting-up and short-distance crawling—are practiced by infants?

When my favorite store has a "Buy One, Get Four Free" sale, my credit cards begin to auto-shuffle in my wallet. My heart palpitates, my palms sweat (unless you believe the old saying: "Horses sweat, men perspire, women glow"), in which case, my palms "glow." I have dizzying visions of numerous tubes and vials of pricey, pale-green cosmetics dancing in my head, or adding whole families to my porcelain Chubby Kid collection.

Have you ever waded through the fine print? "Sale prices exclude: blah, blah, blah,"—followed by half a page of tiny print. They always leave out the good stuff, blaming it on the manufacturer: "Due to manufacturer's requirements . . ." What do they do when they take on these products? Sign a "your stuff will never go on a super-sale" clause? The store should call the shots. If not for the store selling the name-brand merchandise, those pricey labels would be moldering on dusty warehouse shelves.

I'd like to encourage all store managers to throw caution to the winds and have a sale to end all sales. Make the fine print large for Grandma to read without her trifocals and announce an "All the Good Stuff You Ever Wanted to Buy on Sale" sale. Maybe then I could finally finish my Christmas shopping and go out for a cup of plain, black coffee—and a cookie or two.

~ I Hereby Resolve... ~

New Year's resolutions come and go. They usually come in a spurt of insanity on January first and go... around mid-month—if they last that long. Resolutions are seldom taken seriously, they are often entered into on a whim, and they rarely influence the course of our lives—let alone make a significant cosmic blip on the course of history.

I take my role as a north woods native seriously. I try to set an example for all Jackpine Savages (and their Jacqueline counterparts) with whom I come in contact. Therefore, I alert you to the solemnity of carefully selecting New Year's resolutions.

Give generously to area food shelves. I don't plan on being around until the year 3000 (by which time they'll surely be flying to the store, George Jetson-style) and I doubt you'll be here either, so you probably won't need all the canned goods you bought by the truckload in preparation for food shortages. My family can only eat so many meals of creamed corn or string beans doctored-up hotdish style with cream-of-something soup and french-fried onion rings.

Clean house from top to bottom. Imagine how good you'll feel going into the spring-cleaning season, having already completed your cleaning by February. I plan on using those long hibernation months to clean out, sort out, throw out, and give away the flotsam and jetsam of our lives. Then I'll have a suitable stash ready to hold the Garage Sale to end all Garage Sales in the spring.

It's also another way to get rid of your excess stockpile of nearly expired goods. Donate those extra cases of mega-store toilet paper—or start saving bail money for after your teenager giftwraps your entire neighborhood with toilet paper next Halloween. Maybe I'll find a suitable alternate use for Jack's spare generator. (I've discovered it's too big for a doorstop and too unwieldy to use as an anchor for the pontoon.)

Get healthy. In light of entering a shiny new year, wimpy resolutions like losing ten pounds and cutting down on chocolate don't seem momentous enough. I should put my whole family on a health kick—grind my own rosehips and sprinkle them over freshly squeezed orange juice served in sparkling goblets. For those of you I lost back on "grinding rosehips"—no, I'm not taking up exotic dance. Rosehips are the little red buds left on the wild rosebush after the blossoms fall off. The reason they thrive in my yard, since I'm green-thumb-challenged, is because they're wild rosebushes—I have absolutely nothing to do with their success.

Who am I trying to kid? Me? Freshly grind or squeeze anything? Before I've had my morning coffee, I'm so bleary-eyed, I can barely manage to stab the little straw through the hole in a juice box.

Make a budget and stick to it. Okay, here's one I can sink my teeth into. I'm a frugal Scandinavian, whose relatives send coupons in the mail. This spares me the time-consuming task of clipping my own, leaving me free to scour bargain and thrift shops that don't advertise their bargains like normal retail outlets. I love pinching pennies—especially at the grocery store.

If we need barbecue sauce, I'll buy the 128-ounce "Tub-o-Sauce" on sale—even if my family hates that brand. They'll eat it, because every time I *thunk* it on the table in front of their turned-up noses, I remind them what a bargain it was.

The only things I dislike about watching my grocery budget are small technicalities regarding store layout. We know the milk is in the back corner so a shopper on a quick stop for milk has to pass the tempting end-caps first. But why do they put the Slim-Fast across the aisle from the potato chips and pretzels? It's as if they're testing to see how much willpower I possess. When I'm battling the bulge by cutting back on the Ruffles with Ridges, cut me a little slack and put the Slim Fast next to the carrots and celery. At least then I'll have a fighting chance.

Speaking of fighting chances, I think these resolutions are doable. Now that I've written them down, I hope I don't have to eat my words. But if I do I have just the sauce . . .

Computers, Commercials, and the Home Spa Experience

Every new year, I resolve to make a fresh start and clean out my files, whether they need it or not. If you don't write or live with a writer, let me warn you about the significance of every little scrap of paper, even if it only has two or three unintelligible words scribbled on it—it may be valuable fodder for an article. I gather my bits and pieces into a folder and eventually use them to write my stories. I learned early that nothing bad ever happens to a writer. It's all material (thank you, Philip Roth).

Here are a few items of collected flotsam and jetsam. Who knows what ideas will wash up on shore over the next year?

The first item is computer related. Years ago, our oldest sapling was the first one to purchase a computer in our household. I was too busy at the time earning money to pay for things like food, clothes, and his electricity, to use it very often. I went online when he wasn't, which limited my surfing to brief windows of opportunity when he was eating, sleeping, or at school. It was a shock when I realized that, since he was a senior, he would be taking his computer to college. An old Beach Boys tune suddenly flashed into my head: "And she'll have fun, fun, fun, till her son takes his computer away." I had become addicted to checking my email two or three times an hour. Even Big Jack enjoyed it. He and his fellow savages exchanged essential website addresses for places like Outdoors Is Us, the Red Green Show, and Binford Tools.

Over the years, since becoming computer-savvy, I've noticed:

1. The ads on the side of my Facebook page mimic my latest Google search. Not a coincidence.

2. One of the saplings will accidentally disconnect the Wi-fi seconds before I need it.

3. Hotmail doesn't work unless you "accept cookies" under Internet options. I tried deactivating cookies and was blocked from retrieving my mail by the "cookie police." I had to reactivate them. I don't like another computer placing little spies into my computer. Calling them cookies makes them sound cute and harmless, but I know it's an evil plot.

Next, I've decided that one day I'll take a Flip video recorder into the local Mr. Big Burger. I'll have it cued up to replay their latest commercial I recorded from TV. When the camera pans in for a close-up on their juicy, mouthwatering four-and-on-half-inch-high stacked burger masterpiece (carefully constructed by two makeup artists, one French chef, and an Idaho architect), I'll hit the pause button. Showing the freeze-frame of the delectable burger to the flustered teen behind the counter, I'll say, "I'll have one that looks like this—not the one dehydrating under your warming lamps." If he refuses, I'll claim bait-and-switch.

Also, as a newlywed, Jack never complained about my cooking—he was just grateful he didn't have to make dinner. Honestly, he's a better cook than I am at some dishes, but his favorite fare is still meat, potatoes, and meat, with a side of bacon. It used to be hard to get an honest opinion about a new recipe, until I learned to ask, "Shall I make it again?" That brings out the truth every time.

As for health and beauty, I recently saw an article for creating your own home spa experience. Personally, I prefer that my facial ingredients don't consist of the same ingredients—honey, oatmeal, and milk—that toddler Wee Jack used to smear across his face at the breakfast table.

Although I once doctored my hair with a chamomile-tea treatment. I stored it in the refrigerator and forgot to label it. Jack thought it had an odd taste for sun tea, so I just let him think it was an extra-strong batch. I rinsed my hair in it faithfully for a couple of months, then discovered it dried my hair to the consistency of shredded wheat. Perhaps I should have tried it out on Wee Jack's guinea pig first, but someone might have turned me in for resorting to unauthorized animal testing.

If gray hair is supposed to be a crown of splendor and a sign of wisdom, why does my mother keep sending me Loving Care coupons? Does she know something I don't?

And vitamins will help us achieve healthy, more-productive lives. Have you seen the commercials for One-a-Day? They've invented different combinations to help with conditions like memory and concentration, tension and mood, energy, and sex appeal. How do I decide which one to take? I need them all.

Northern Comfort

It's time to stock up on the essential ingredients for my winter-survival kit: chocolate, coffee, and popcorn. While I'd never make it through a long winter's night without chocolate and coffee, popcorn is in a special class all by itself. How many other snack foods are as versatile? When your driveway is buried under three feet of snow and boredom sets in, popcorn easily makes the transition from table to home-decorating craft item—unlike its snacking counterparts, which are merely edible. (Have you ever seen a potato chip garland?)

Popcorn is comfort food—complete with the familiar popcorn-making ritual. For some unknown reason, it pops best in the crustiest-looking heavy kettle, with matching, equally crusty lid. Every north woods kitchen worth its popcorn salt should have an official Popcorn Pan, etched with years of fond memories and permanently baked-on grease that no Brillo pad could ever remove.

Popcorn is also festive party fare. What other food item could call itself "Orville Redenbacher's," and be taken seriously? The name itself can hardly be uttered without at least cracking a smile. We all remember being around a campfire as children, eagerly vying with our siblings or camping buddies to take our turn to shake the Jiffy-Pop. There was something almost magical about watching it puff up its foil-domed lid. (The Jiffy-Pop people now have a disclaimer on the package, claiming it should only be popped on a stovetop. I have one hyphenated word for that—popcorn-party-pooper.)

When I was a freshman in college—a few years before the invention of the microwave—I was eager to treat my dormmates by christening the new electric popcorn popper I'd received as a graduation gift. I walked to the nearest grocery store and purchased popcorn supplies. Returning to my room, I carefully measured the ingredients, put them in the popper, and turned it on. We all waited hungrily for the wafting scent of popping corn to fill the air.

Instead, we began to detect a scorched, burnt aroma—nothing at all resembling freshly popped corn.

"Maybe it's just burning off the newness," I suggested. The noxious odor increased, along with a few vaporous wisps of smoke. "I know it shouldn't be doing that." I yanked the plug from the outlet and removed the lid. Inside was a crusty-looking mass of black, scorched popcorn kernels glued to the bottom of the popper.

Instead of corn oil, I had hastily purchased corn syrup.

I chiseled out as much of the black mass as I could, soaked the inside of the popcorn popper for a couple of weeks, and finally relegated it to the dumpster. I recently learned that one of the ingredients of the famed Kettle Korn—found at fairs and flea markets—is corn syrup. How do they get away with it?

My dentist's wife once told me she never eats popcorn because the hulls are too hard to get out from between her teeth. How can anyone not eat popcorn? It's as American as apple pie, Thanksgiving turkey, and going to the movies. Put out some fresh popcorn and everyone in the house eventually gravitates to the bowl, helping themselves with gusto to its buttery, salted crunch. If Jack starts a batch of microwave popcorn after Wee Jack has gone to bed, W.J. calls down the steps, "Save me some popcorn!" And if W.J. gets up before I do the next morning, he is already munching contentedly from his popcorn stash, watching cartoons. I think popcorn-flavored breakfast cereal would go over big at our house.

Candied popcorn balls, nestled in crinkly red, green, or gold cellophane, herald the advent of the Christmas season. A few always make their way into my shopping cart, along with a bag of popcorn kernels to pop for the garland to drape festively around the family Christmas tree. I'm surprised someone hasn't tried to market fake popcorn to trim the tree—either strings of lightbulbs shaped like popped corn or plastic popcorn garland—they could even make it popcorn-scented.

Popcorn even has its own website, complete with dozens of recipes. Try one when the winds howl and the snow piles itself around your eaves. Just remember to purchase corn *oil*.

~ Power to the People- ~
~ Watching ~

People-watching is one of my favorite pastimes. I'll always remember a remark I overheard years ago in the produce aisle of a Couer d'Alene, Idaho, grocery store. Two soccer moms were chatting, and one of them remarked that her daughter's school uniform "looked like a cross between Mary Poppins and the Virgin Mary." For years, I've tried to picture what that looked like.

A prime venue for people watching has been severely curtailed since 9/11. Airports used to be a great place for watching passengers in varying degrees of dress and/or meltdown. Now only those with boarding passes are allowed beyond the security screening area—which leaves all the really good people watching for those taking flight themselves.

One winter, Jack and I escaped for a week in sunny Florida. At the first boarding gate, after passing through security, we listened to the comments of passengers who hadn't been waved through as quickly as we were. Shoes were checked, including a black, clunky platform pair worn by a waif-like teenage girl. And a chunky thirty-something man boisterously announced to his traveling partners—and more than a hundred strangers—how much he enjoyed his patdown.

Our treatment at the airport was less invasive. We don't fit The Profile and luckily were not randomly selected to have our persons and possessions searched or wanded. Watching the look on Jack's face while he endured a patdown would almost have been worth the inconvenience. He already felt half-dressed without his trusty jackknife in his pocket. I remembered to remove my tweezers and nail clippers from the carry-on bag and place them in the checked luggage. I also debated switching the eyelash curler, but decided to leave it in the makeup kit. Curling didn't seem to be an immediate threat to airline security.

I read a newspaper column written by a woman who didn't think she fit any of the profiles either. But her unusual, work-generated travel plans meant her tickets were purchased late, she changed airlines partway through her itinerary, and her final destination was not reached by a direct flight. Despite her harmless and innocent appearance, she was pulled aside as soon as she approached the first security checkpoint and was red-flagged to be searched many times before she reached her ultimate destination.

After a week spent enjoying sun and sand, we were back at the airport. A teenage girl who seemed proud of her tan was returning to Minnesota wearing a skin-tight white tanktop that left nothing to the imagination. While I was thinking, *Those parents have their hands full*, I heard Jack murmur, "No daughter of mine would be allowed to wear that out in public." Good thing we have sons. Boys' clothing isn't nearly as inflammatory.

A family deplaned with a five-year-old girl who was pulling her own carry-on bag. When she asked, "When are we in Florida?" Her dad replied as though in a stupor, "We're in Florida now." His dazed expression made me wonder how many times she'd asked that question.

There were myriad pairs of parents juggling two sets of strollers and carseats. Along with the same number of diaper bags and backpacks, they also wrangled at least two tired, squalling (and in dire need of a bath and/or diaper change) infants or toddlers who necessitated the need for enough gear to mobilize a tiny-tots army. And that didn't count what they had stowed in the hold of the plane's luggage compartment.

I wished my camera was accessible when we saw a wiry National Guard soldier fully dressed in camouflage. He strode purposefully down the concourse, carrying a forgotten fluffy pink snowsuit to the loading gate. He'd left his post at the passenger screening station to make sure a little girl would be warmly dressed when she arrived in Minnesota. After 9/11, we had grown accustomed to the news reports of stony-faced guardsmen at the nation's airports, whose forbidding expressions rivaled those of the guards at Buckingham Palace. It was a heartwarming glimpse of a kinder, gentler military.

And an airline employee—seeing a half-finished baby bottle on her check-in counter—glimpsed the family it belonged to heading down the concourse. She made two announcements over the intercom: "Will the party who forgot the baby bottle on the counter return and pick it up." The young parents, pushing two children in strollers and draped with countless bags, were oblivious to the intercom's message. Though she wasn't supposed to leave her post, the employee scurried down the concourse with the bottle in hand and returned it to the family.

While prime people watching occurs when flying the friendly skies, the north woods also offers many rewarding opportunities. If you see me pull out a notepad and pen, I may or may not be jotting a grocery list—but I'll never tell.

No, I Have the Sexiest Man Alive

I don't follow much pop culture, but I did catch a recent headline that someone named Bradley Cooper just beat out Ryan Gosling for *People* magazine's "Sexiest Man Alive" award. I must admit at first I thought that "Gosling" was the father of the *Kate+Eight* kids, but then I remembered that is another G name: Gosselin. Thinking Gosselin had won the award is what prompted me to read beyond the headline. Yeah, I know you didn't think it would be him either.

All that being said, they still got it wrong.

The winner of the Sexiest Man Alive is my own Jackpine Savage husband.

Yes, we've had a few thorns in our bed of roses and our "for better or for worse" have been tested a few times, but I wouldn't trade him for all the *People* magazine picks, past, present, or future.

He takes home the honors for being the faithful man I married thirty-seven years ago. He never fails to make me laugh (and sometimes groan) with his unassuming wit and few, but effective, words. Who else could say in all seriousness that there are wild concubines all over the yard? Uh, honey, I think you meant "columbines."

He is also the King of Being Prepared. Have you seen his hat or boot collection? Something for any season, any event, any reason—amazing! He took his Cub Scout/Boy Scout/Eagle Scout badges seriously and he's the one I'd want around if my life depended on it or even if it didn't.

He works hard, and he hunts and fishes to stock our freezer. Just as he did with our older ones, he chauffeured our youngest sapling to games, practices, youth group, or 7:00 a.m. band class, and attended as many events as possible. He enjoys watching others perform their sports, art, or music, and is amazed at the blessings of grandchildren. He especially loves his family and cares deeply about their lives.

One of his unsung claims to fame is that he's a really good cook. He did most of the cooking, and even shopping and cleaning while I finished my degrees. He supports the extra time I put in as a part-time professor, and he has called out "Supper's ready," far more than I have lately.

He is a stalwart, godly man. And when I need them, his shoulders are even big enough to cry on.

I consider all of those qualities very sexy.

I could go on, but I think you get the general idea.

How could pretty boys Cooper or Gosling ever measure up to that? Yeah . . . I thought so.

North Woods Notes

Snowplow Perspective

Our son and his family came home from the city for the weekend. We had received very little snow all winter, so when the weather reports forecasted snow, we didn't expect much accumulation. As the snow continued to pile up, he realized they were unable to leave. State, county, and private plows all needed to work in synch to clear our roads of snow.

"How long will you stay?" I asked my son, as we watched the snow continue to fall.

"We'll stay till the plows come home," he replied, with a twinkle in his eye.

A Snug Fit

My sister, another veteran bargain hunter, and I love scavenging together at garage sales. A few years ago, we used our bargain-hunting skills to pick up gently used items for my last baby. Perusing the wares at one sale, she on one side of the garage, me on the other, she called out to get my attention over the heads of the other shoppers.

"Do you need a snuggie?" Sara shouted. As all heads swiveled to look her way, I saw her holding aloft a soft-fabric child carrier. Choking back laughter, I hastily made my way around the tables to her side and replied, "No, I don't need a "snuggie," but I could use a "Snugli!"

On the Road Again

I knew one of my job descriptions was chauffeur, but I didn't realize our sons noticed the amount of time I spent shuttling them to their various sports practices and events.

On yet another trek to the ski hill, following a busy fall of one cross-country running practice and meet after another, my oldest sapling summed it up. "Mom, you have a new winter sport—cross-country driving."

Dog Food

A well-meaning relative once suggested that since I like to write and I like dogs, perhaps I should write dog food advertisements. My sister-in-law overheard and saw my expression of distaste.

She summed it up nicely: "You have to write about what inspires you—all the rest is just dog food."

Four Seasons

Jack's conversation often revolves around his upcoming fall hunting trips. We didn't realize the effect this was having on our two sapling sons, then five and three years old. One evening, he read a bedtime story to the boys. The story was about a cat that learned the four seasons: spring, summer, fall, and winter.

When he finished, Jack asked the boys, "Now can you tell me the seasons?"

"Sure, Daddy," replied the oldest. Without missing a beat, he recited, "Duck season, goose season, moose season, and deer season."

Friend for All Seasons

We share a lot, my friend.
We breathe life into dreams grown cold from neglect,
pose not-quite earth-shattering solutions
to current events,
voice quieter fears of aging and Alzheimer's.

These appear so monumental in comparison.

It's fall, you see,
and I really need to know—
How many zucchini can our friendship take?

Wardrobe Malfunctions: Thoughts from the Heartland

Since when did plumber's butt become high fashion? There is no longer a fine, *ahem*, line between de rigueur [*Webster's: required by etiquette; according to good form; proper*] and derriere.

I was recently at a large church garage sale and witnessed a portly young woman who was dressed in a belly shirt and low-rider jeans. With no concern for the body parts she had on display and irrespective of those around her, she was bent over, sorting through a box of purses. Her rear end waggled in the air, buns threatening to burst, literally, from their seams.

Since I was on my last round of the sale area, I was carrying a comforter and a large piece of tweedy plaid material. My hands nearly twitched with the effort it took to restrain myself from swathing her in fabric. From the sidelong glances of others, I could tell I was not alone. I finally murmured, not too softly, to another onlooker, "I keep wanting to drape something over that posterior." The woman nodded in agreement.

Keep it under wraps in the north woods . . .

Open, Sesame!

It was my first visit to the service department of the local, brand-spanking-new car dealership. From the curved, arched roof soaring regally over the automatic-eye-activated garage doors, to the floor-to-ceiling crystal-blue showroom windows— it was a state-of-the-art, architectural masterpiece.

After turning my car over to the service technician, and marveling at their white-tiled floors, I stopped at the parts department for a car seat locking clip. Pausing in front of the glass panel, I waited for the automatic door to slide aside. When it didn't budge, I glanced around for a manual over-ride button. Then I saw the real door, complete with old-fashioned handles, to my left. Expecting something more "high-tech," I'd been waiting in front of a window.

In sixth grade, our son learned in school that the body fat of an athlete in peak condition was a mere 6.6 percent.

"My fat count will never be that low," I moaned.

Trying to make me feel better, my husband remarked, "You're not that bad, honey. You just have untoned mush-el."

Forget about It!

On countless schooldays, my third-grade sapling forgot something at home: a mitten, his homework, a library book, the list seemed never-ending.

But one March morning, as I backed the car out of the driveway, I said, "I have the feeling I'm forgetting something."

He quickly shot back, "Welcome to my world."

Sweets for the Sweet

The good thing about finding an empty candy wrapper in the dryer after washing my sapling's clothes, is knowing I won't find a melted chocolate bar stuck to the wash load. No candy bar can survive that long in his possession.

When Teen Jack claims that our car is his, I have just the answer to stop him in his car tracks. I've threatened to get a vanity plate: *ITSMOMS*.

Heaven forbid, if we ever had a house fire, I know our faithful Lab would save us. She'd wake us up to wave a towel at the smoke detector like we do when dinner is ready.

❧ • ☙

One Tweet Year (selected Twitter randomness)

A 5,500-year-old shoe was discovered in an Armenia cave. I'm sure its mate is along a highway somewhere.

In home decor circles, is having too many fridge magnets similar to having too many cats?

The secret of not sharing my lunchbox with Teen Jack is ditching basic black & getting a pink girly model.

Shouldn't animal crackers contain protein?

Trying to decide if we're violating Child Labor laws or Sweatshop ordinances when we make our children play baseball when it's eighty-six-plus degrees.

Saw a dead crow on the hiway. Two other crows were attempting to finish him off. Lends new meaning to: We leave no fallen soldier behind.

What is this editor supposed to think when the manuscript wings its way to my hands via a Homer Simpson's stamp?

A "fishing camp" was set up at a cabin on our road. Budweiser Welcome Fishermen sign & trucks/boats. Do I tell them the opener is next week?

Motel 6 gets a makeover. Now where do I go to teach my kids the meaning of a "dive"? #sturgiscamping #blackhills

Inhalable coffee is being touted as "the kick of coffee without the cup" Gotta . . . get . . . some . . . now!

Headline reads: "Coyote nabbed in the wilds of New York City." NYC has "wilds?" Must be the block w/out a Starbucks.

Re: Lady Gaga attire—As my sister used to say in the 1960s, "Let's not and say we did!"

Got four emails from PR firm representing someone claiming to be: The World Record Holder in Memory. Must have forgotten the first three sends.

How can a TV ad speak to someone who "may have died" from a treatment and think they are reaching the target audience?

Tried to wipe off an over-abundance of hair product, then realized that it was the gray at my temples. #isgrayhairreallyacrown?

Wouldn't you think that the average, run-of-the-mill spam filter would be smart enough to toss out anything with viagra in the subject line?

On to more important news: bubble wrap is fifty years old! Did you know it started as an idea for wallpaper?

In the "too-weird" department: Holiday Inn Offers "Human Bed-Warming Service" to Combat Icy Sheets

Someday I want to pull up the bing.com photo of the day, call an airline, and book a flight to that exotic destination.

I wish I had a list of all the brilliant thoughts I have just before falling asleep.

One flight in not-so-friendly skies: medical emergency, child kicking seat, loud, crude woman, prisoner in handcuffs. Think I'll drive.

The Detroit airplane terrorist's incendiary method lends new meaning to: "Don't get your undies in a bunch . . ."

If we had to remove shoes for airport security after the Shoe Bomber, now this new terrorist sewed the bomb material in his underwear . . .

Does anyone else think it's a bit unnerving when your computer takes over to run an update and you had no clue that it's happening?

Fondly remembers schoolbus days: "Who lit the firecracker?!"

Friend attending a webinar during work hours. I quickly read note & thought it said winebar. Same letters/different deal. Letdown.

How did we Boomers survive our infancies? We had no bilirubin lights for jaundice, we were given aspirin, and we slept on our tummies!

It must be fun to say you're from Wahoo, Nebraska.

What is the universe trying to tell me when my Dove chocolate doesn't have a message inside the wrapper?

I agree with a friend that the roller coaster of life could use safety belts.

THE END